Gifts of Onile

Gifts of Onile

"A Tombigbee Tale"

Eddie J. Carr

AuthorHouse™
1663 Liberty Drive
Bloomington, IN 47403
www.authorhouse.com
Phone: 1-800-839-8640

Published by AuthorHouse 01/14/2013

ISBN: 978-1-4817-0336-9 (sc)
ISBN: 978-1-4817-0335-2 (e)

Library of Congress Control Number: 2012924286

This book is printed on acid-free paper.

Contents

Chapter 1

HORSE HUNTING

The cork bobbed and Josh reached for the pole he had stuck in the sand. The coolness of the creek slowly passing by helped to ease the heat on the muggy June morning. The dew was almost gone with the sun drying it up. He played with the fish on the line a little before pulling it in and placing it on a limb with several that he had already caught. Josh sat and began to think about his paw. It was 1866 and the war had been over for almost a year. They had received no word from him in several months and his maw feared the worse. Josh could remember his paw leaving and with Josh being nineteen at the time, he wanted to go with his dad to fight in the war but stayed at the ranch to help his mother try and keep things going at his dads urging. Josh was now twenty-two, and stood around six foot three. He was a handsome man in many a young girl's eye, with his curly black hair and brown eyes. He had broad shoulders and a muscular build from working the fields and cattle.

The ranch set on a little over twenty eight hundred acres near the town of St. Stephens, Alabama. What use to be a thriving town and the first state capitol wasn't much of a town anymore. It had given way to progress and larger towns like Jackson and Mount Vernon, but there were still some folks that lived there. Jonathan Wilkes, Josh's dad, had claimed the land through a lottery. He drew a number and had a certain amount of time to mark the land with his own stakes. He was able to get land by the Tombigbee River which was good for growing crops and raising cattle. It had four creeks running through it. As a matter of fact most of the land was bordered by the river. Josh was much like his dad when it came to work because he didn't mind it. He had been taught by his paw, how to take care of his maw and himself. In keeping his hopes alive, Josh worked hard doing all he could to keep the ranch going until is paw come back home.

Josh reached to grab the pole for another fish when he heard the rustling of the brush and could hear the sound of horses coming in his direction. The creek had a ten foot embankment and as Josh turned he saw a large bay horse come over the edge of the bluff and down the slope. Just as that bays head dropped a lasso missed catching nothing but air then dropped to the ground. Behind the big bay were two salty looking soldiers. Josh had seen them before, out trying to round up wild strays for the Cavalry to ride and fight Indians out west. The soldiers had some pretty choice words as the big bay bounded across that creek in about three leaps and stopped on the other side. The horse looked back as if he was waiting on them and wondering why they had stopped. He was seemingly unhappy that the chase had ended. After sitting atop the embankment a few seconds, the two soldiers turned away grumbling and vowing to catch the horse on another day.

The creek was plenty shallow where the big bay had crossed, no more than twenty to thirty feet wide and a couple feet deep. The horse pawed the ground a couple of times then looked around at Josh. He again pawed the ground and snorted tossing his head back and forth, his black mane slapping each side of his neck. The horse stood might near sixteen hands and was bay in color. He had two white sox on the right side and black on the left. The star in the middle of his forehead was not ordinary as it was more a diamond shape. He appeared healthy for a horse in the wild and looked to be fast. Josh stood there looking when all of a sudden the horse spun around and took off up the sand bar, over the embankment and back into the woods. Josh leaned over and grabbed the pole that he had dropped when he herd the sounds coming his way. The fish was still flopping around on the ground. He placed the fish with the ones he had and got on his horse to start back to the ranch. As he mounted, he knew without a doubt that he wanted that big bay horse and somehow, someway, he was going to get him. He sat there looking back at where he saw the horse last standing, pondering what it would be like to have such a magnificent animal, then turned and headed home.

WIJA Shaunti was a young black man nineteen years old. He was about six feet tall and was stout and muscular.

He really had no country to speak of except Africa where his mom and dad came from. His mom, Zuri, and dad, Edonta, had been captured by a rival tribe and sold to slave traders. Zuri was pregnant when they were captured and Wija was born on the ship during the crossing. In 1847, they were placed on the auction block in Mobile, Alabama and Edonta was bought by Mr. Jonathan Wilkes. It wasn't until after Mr. Wilkes had purchased Edonta that he found out Zuri and Wija were to be sold together and that Zuri was Edonta's wife. Mr. Wilkes was a fair and honest man and he couldn't let that family be separated. He began bidding on the two and had stiff competition from a neighbor of his, a big plantation owner, Clarence Ruffkin, who was said to be abusive to slaves. It took Mr. Wilkes deeding twenty-five acres of land to Ruffkin to get him to stop bidding so that Jonathan could keep the family together. Mr. Wilkes spent most of the money he had but was able to keep them as a family and on that day Edonta and Zuri swore to be faithful to the Wilkes family. Since they had been with the Wilkes, they had two more children born to them, a boy Enu, (second born) and Adia (beautiful). Enu was fifteen and Adia thirteen. Their life was one of work but they did not have to worry about abuse, Mr. Wilkes gave them ten acres of land for themselves and they worked with him and Josh in the fields and with the cattle. They had freedoms that most slaves didn't have until the emancipation and were never considered as slaves by the Wilkes family. They were treated as family and they were loyal to the Wilkes family.

The only other person on the farm was Old Tim, (Jaborni), a slave that had walked away from his plantation when all slaves were freed. Tim had a good reason for not venturing to far from the ranch. He had been beaten up pretty bad by a mob in Jackson. Mrs. Wilkes found him lying in the street and loaded him on a buckboard bringing him back to the ranch. Zuri and Mrs. Wilkes tended him back to health and he had been on the ranch every since. He wore an eye patch over his left eye cause he lost it in the beating he took. He was a heck of a worker and he knew about animals. That was his main purpose on the ranch and he worked hard at it. It was felt that Tim would never leave the ranch because he felt safe there and looking at all the scars, he had been through some pretty tough times. Tim was somewhere around fifty five although he wasn't real sure of his age. The plantation he came from was down around New Orleans. In leaving the plantation he was hoping to make a better life for himself. He worked at training horses for running at a track down there and he sure had ways of working animals, no matter what kind.

Wija had just finished up helping his dad, Edonta; store some corn in the crib when he saw Josh coming up the road. He walked out to meet him and see how the morning had been. Wija's best friend was Josh and even though he could leave the farm any time he wanted, he would very seldom stray far without Josh nearby. They had grown up together and in spirit were like brothers. Besides, he had heard stories about how slaves had been treated and so far his life had been peaceful.

Josh was all excited and began to tell Wija about the big bay horse and what had happened down by the creek. Josh let it be known that he was going to have that horse and Wija felt that he would do whatever it took to get him. Wija knew he would be talking to air but he made it a point to explain to Josh that they had plenty of horses on the ranch already broke and ready to ride but Josh would have none of it. Josh kept repeating over and over that this horse was special, that there was something about him and the way he acted.

Wija looked at Josh and said "Okay, we will find this horse, now do you mind if we get them fish cleaned for supper."

Josh looked disgruntled and said, "Ya don't believe me?"

Wija told him that he did believe him but his maw ain't waiting on them to catch no horse, she'd probably like to get them fish fried before they dry rot." Giving up for now, Josh handed the fish to Wija.

That evening after supper Edonta and Zuri had gone to their cabin along with Adia. Enu was sitting on the end of the porch playing a spiritual tune on his harmonica. Old Tim had a small cabin to himself but you never knew if he was in it or not. He would spend some nights in the woods in back of it or either sleep in the loft at the barn. It was kind of felt that Tim was afraid to be trapped in that cabin in case some one came after him. Most of the time you wouldn't find him in there unless it was bad weather or in the winter. The evening was cool as Josh and Wija sat on the porch. Their conversation was about the horse. It ended up that Wija made a pact with Josh that he would help him find and catch the horse but with a condition. Josh, not knowing what to expect, reluctantly said "Okay." Wija told Josh that once they got the horse, he wanted to name him. Seemed easy enough so Josh agreed to the terms and they shook on it. Wija headed across the yard towards the cabin and Josh asked him what kind of name he had in mind.

Wija turned around and grinned saying, "Once we catch the horse I'll know and then you will know."

Several weeks past and work on the ranch was laboring and tiring. Neither Josh nor Wija had time to stop for anything. They worked from sun up to sun down and ached when they would go to bed at night. Tim was working the cattle, branding and raising new born calfs, working the horses and keeping up with the chickens and hogs. Edonta, Josh, Wija and Enu was bringing in crops and helping with the animals as much as they could. Mrs. Wilkes, Zuri and Adia were busy canning vegetables and fruits for the winter months along with cleaning and cooking for four hungry men. Josh had not forgot the horse and thought about ways to catch him when and if he could find the time to do it. That wasn't all that Josh had on his mind. There was still no word from his dad and even though it was hard, Josh had the feeling that his dad wouldn't be returning.

Alicia Wilkes would not give up on her husband returning. Many an evening she sat in her rocking chair watching the road and waiting on him to come walking down it. The war had taken many a good man but for some reason she could still feel Jonathan in her being. She could feel him alive and trying to get home even though it had been a year. She was a strong woman and as pretty as a woman could be, but the past few years had taken a toll on her. She was struggling to keep the ranch going even with the help of Edonta's family. She wished so desperately for her husband to come home and take over even though she knew Josh could handle things. As for Josh, he knew his ma and he knew that no other man would ever take his paws place, and there had been some who tried. They didn't know how his paw felt about things like that, he always said, "You don't go trying to stir a man's pot while he is away or you may not be asked to supper."

Near the end of July some of the crops and cattle had been sold but not nearly what Josh and his maw had hoped for. They would get the money needed for land taxes when the fall crops and cattle were sold but for now they was just shy of what they needed. In all though Josh felt pretty good being able to raise the money needed. Before they knew it next spring would be here and the cycle would start again. So for now it was time for Josh and Wija to set out and find that horse, if it wasn't too late. After completing their daily chores, the two would set out and had been searching everywhere they could think of where that horse may be. They had staked out several locations where they knew the herd that roamed the area would travel but after three weeks, hadn't seen hide or hair of em. Then one afternoon while heading back to the ranch they saw some soldiers crossing the Ruffkin plantation with about ten to twelve horses. Josh knew strait away that one of the horses was the big bay. He knew because there were three ropes around that horses' neck and he was acting up something fierce. He was kicking and jumping and the soldier's that was holding onto the ropes had their hands full.

Josh grabbed Wija by the arm and pointed to the soldiers and horses. Josh said "The one with all those ropes, that's the big bay I was telling you about."

"That is the one you want?" asked Wija?

Josh said, "Yep, ain't he something?"

Wija looked at Josh as if he had lost his mind and then said "Yeah, something to get your self killed on." They rode towards the soldiers and Josh struck up a conversation with the sergeant.

"Afternoon sir," Josh said "Looks like you've got some pretty rank ones there." The sergeant snarled and said, "Yea but we will handle them soon enough." Josh was just trying to make conversation and asked him what they were going to do with the wild one in the back. The sergeant looked at him as if Josh was being a bother and said, "Well we will break him or put a bullet in his head." Trying to think of what to say next, Josh hadn't noticed that Wija had walked back to the horse and was calmly talking to him. Both the sergeant and Josh noticed quietness and turned to look to see what was going on. Wija had dismounted and walked over to where the soldiers were struggling with the horse. He stood calmly within a few feet of the horse. The horse had stopped rearing and kicking and was steadily looking at this person coming near to him. Wija spoke softly and the horse seemed to relax. He walked slowly up to the big bay and began stroking him on the neck. The horse snorted some and shook his head but Wija stood his ground speaking softly to him. Wija was staring into the horses eyes and concentrating on the animal's behavior.

It was only a few seconds before the sergeant yelled at Wija to get away from the horse. Josh wasn't sure if it was because of Wija's color or how easily he got that horse to calm down. Wija complied and eased away and got back on his horse. No more than a second after Wija had walked a way, the horse started giving the soldiers fits again. The sergeant asked Wija what he had done to the horse.

Wija said, "I did nothing to harm the horse, I spoke with him. He looked at the sergeant and said that horse will not be tamed by anger." It was obvious that the sergeant didn't care too much for Wija and told him that if they couldn't tame the horse then they would put a bullet in his head. The sergeant gave his soldiers orders to continue on with the horses and there was no doubt that those three handling the big bay would be tired when they go home.

As the sergeant turned to ride off Josh stopped him "Sir would you consider giving me that horse?"

Without hesitation the sergeant said "No way." "We have been after that horse for months. He has spirit and I think we can make a fine Cavalry horse out of him."

Again, Wija spoke and said "You will not tame that horse by anger; Onile will not be trained by those who would harm him."

The sarge looked at Wija and asked "How the hell do you know and what is Onile?"

Wija said "I know because he told me and Onile is from my native country language, it means "Spirit of the

Land." You will try but you will not tame him." The sarge turned his horse and rode off.

Josh and Wija headed back to the house. Josh was not about to give up on getting that horse. He looked at Wija and asked "Him how he knew that the horse wouldn't be tamed?"

Wija corrected Josh, "I did not say that he would not be tamed; I said they would not tame him by anger", as he spoke with his native accent.

"How you know/", asked Josh and to his surprise Wija said, "The horse told me."

Wija continued, "I looked into his eyes, he is a strong horse with a spirit, pride and he is strong to protect those he cares for in his herd. This is why they will not tame him, he will not be controlled by anger and they have a lot of it, those who will try to tame him are full of hate and it is not good for them or the horse."

Josh looked puzzled and ask, "You seen all that by looking into his eyes?

Wija replied "Yes."

Josh smiled to himself and Wija asked him why he was amused at such a thing?

Josh said "Well if you saw all of that by just looking into his eyes, then maybe you should have a word with that old bull back at the house, tell me what he has to say about things!" They both laughed out loud then Josh said "Onile, it is."

Chapter 2

WORKING A DEAL

It was cool for an August evening. After supper Joshua sat on the porch cleaning his gun, a forty five Colt, his dad had left him for protection in case of problems. He had been taught how to use it and had practiced a lot making himself pretty good with it. He had never been challenged so he didn't know what would happen if he had to draw and shoot, but he could hit anything he aimed at. His maw didn't care too much for him having it but inside she knew it might be a need one day. She also knew that his father had taught Josh how and when to use it if he needed too and how to be responsible.

The kerosene lantern was aided by the light of a full moon which had stirred up two owls screeching in the night. It also brought sadness to Alicia. Josh could see the reflection of tears on her cheeks. He knew she was thinking about paw and only wished he knew how to console her and make her feel better. After sitting silently for several minutes Josh started to speak hoping to get her mind headed into another direction.

Mom, Wija and I saw that big bay horse I been telling you about? The Army had captured him and had ropes all over him and that horse was giving them fits. I don't know what it is about him but I sure do like that horse and I just got to figure out a way to get him. He told her of the events that afternoon and how Wija calmed that horse down and how the soldiers treated Wija. Wija told them they would not tame the horse with anger and they seemed to get mad about that too.

Alicia looked at her son and knew that he had started the conversation to get her mind off Jonathan. She said, "Wija has been learning a lot about animals from Tim and he has learned well, it does not surprise me that he handled the horse in such a manner."Josh, if they captured that horse, you may have to realize that they won't give him away. If it is meant to be then you will have him, the lord will provide a way for it. As for how they acted towards Wija, you need to remember that most of those soldiers fought in the war and many of them came from the south. They still have hard feelings about colored and they are not ready to accept them as being equal. You must be mindful of this and careful when you and Wija are out there. "It will take time for things to heal but they will in time."

Josh looked at her and said, "Yeah mom, things will heal with time," hoping that she would know he was speaking of paw." "I know folks haven't accepted things yet and some of them are just plain mean." He then assured her he would be careful. Josh made sure to keep talking about other things and didn't mention his paw. It was quiet and they sit in silence for a while listening to Zuri's voice coming from their cabin. She was singing some Negro spiritual songs that were sung in the fields while they worked. Edonta and Adia would join in and the sound was pleasant and relaxing. Alicia retired into the house and Josh finished cleaning the gun. He again found himself thinking of the horse. The moon dropped behind the trees and Josh doused the lantern and went to bed.

The dim morning light awakened Josh and he could hear the rooster crowing. He rolled out of bed and got dressed. The smell of bacon and coffee being cooked by Zuri had stirred up his appetite. Walking to the kitchen Josh could see his mom talking with Tim in the backyard. Tim had a look of concern on his face which was not a common thing. His mom also seemed to be fretting over what ever it was but Josh knew if it was important she would tell him. They both came into the house and sat down at the table. A blessing was given for the food and then as they began to eat, they discussed the things needed to be done for the day. Alicia spoke first and told Josh to take Wija and go with Tim. "Y'all will need to help him mend a fence that had been torn down near the river side of the south draw. Tim will go with you and show you where it is at. We lost some cattle last night and I want you to see if you can find out where they went." As she was talking Josh noticed the worry in her eyes. From her looks, he felt that she was worried about more than the fence being down.

Tim spoke up and said, "Yeah, it looks like the fence was cut and them cattle stole."

Mrs. Wilkes cautioned him about being hasty on assuming that they had been taken by rustlers, the cows may have just busted the fence down.

"Don't think so missy," Tim said, "Wire looked to have been cut and I am staking that we have some thieves around here."

Josh promised to check it out and if he found what Tim said to be true he and Wija would ride to town and let the sheriff know. He was itching to go and see what was going on with the horse anyway. Alicia again warned him to be careful.

The three of them Josh, Wija and Tim, rode to the south draw and looked at the fence. The ends of the wire had apparently been cut and several head of cattle pushed through the opening by at least four or five horses. They were moved out towards the Ruffkin plantation. The fence was repaired and while fixing it, Wija noticed some blood on the ground near the opening where the wire had been cut. Somebody had been cut by the barbs on the wire and it looked like they had been cut pretty bad. Wija pointed out that the person would have cuts to his arm or hands by the looks of the amount of blood but then again it could have been one of the cows. Josh suggested they ride to town and let Sheriff Duncan know. Tim was still leery about going to Jackson so he decided to check on how many head of cattle may have been taken while Josh and Wijja headed to town which was a good seven miles away.

Once they arrived in town, Josh made the report to Sheriff Duncan. Duncan was a short man in his late forties. Some say he had served time for beating a man to death over a woman up in Montgomery. His time was cut short because a witness had come forward and told the truth about what had happened that night. Duncan was released from prison and just to make sure he wouldn't get into anymore trouble and that nobody got accused falsely for something they didn't do, he turned to keeping the peace. He moved to Jackson and took over the job after the previous sheriff had retired. Seemed to be doing a good job and was known to be good with his fist and guns. Sheriff Duncan listened to Josh and assured him that he would look into it and keep his ear to the ground to see what he could find out.

As they headed out of town Josh and Wija ran into Clarence Ruffkin and his niece Christine. Josh never cared to much for Ruffkin a man who owned about half of the county, but he was always cordial to him. Ruffkins' plantation covered some four thousand acres and he owned more land in the adjoining county. There was rumors that he got a lot of his money from some slave ships that he had financed out of Mobile, but no one knew for sure. What was for sure was now he had no slaves to work his plantation, he had gone to cutting timber to make money. He was supposedly from a French family that had settled down in Mobile. Ruffkin was in his late fifties, didn't have any accent that Josh could tell of yet he was a strong looking fellow. He had a scar on his right cheek which he is said to have gotten from a duel with a man that had insulted his family. The duel was with swords and he killed the man, giving him a fair reputation as being able to take care of himself. He had never married but could have many times.

Christine was Clarence's sister's daughter. She was sent to him after his sister had died of malaria in Charleston South Carolina. Her dad had been killed at Vicksburg and she had no one else to tend to her so Ruffkin took her in and gave her a place to live. She had been with him for several years. She was twenty years of age and had black hair and dark brown eyes. She was wearing some close fitting jeans and a white and blue checkered button up blouse that she filled out quiet well. Josh felt she was mighty pretty and if not for Ruffkin, he would have already called on her. Josh nodded to them as he passed, keeping his eyes on her all the way. She smiled at him and it sent butterflies through him. The horse was the first thing on his mind but she filled that space pretty fast especially when she spoke. Her voice was pleasant and nice to listen too.

After speaking to them, Josh and Wija headed down the street but Josh noticed Mr. Ruffkin was watching them as they rode off. When Josh had told him of the cattle being stolen, Ruffkin acted as if they had made the story up. It should have concerned him since his land was the land that the rustlers had to come across to get the cattle. According to Ruffkin, he had not seen or heard anything from his hands about any strangers on his property. Christine was fixing to speak and Ruffkin cut her off real quick and told Josh that he would keep his eye out and tell him if he saw or heard anything. Josh had the feeling, the way Ruffkin was watching them and acting strange, that he did know something. Josh and Wija both noticed and Josh also noticed Christine looking at him.

Quiet a gal Wija said, too bad her uncle ain't so friendly.

Josh said, "I am not interested in him anyway."

As they started out of town, they could see the corrals the Army had placed the horses in. They were just outside Fort Colman's gate. There were two of them and one had several horses in it. The other was empty except for one horse and one soldier. A soldier was breaking the horse and had pretty much conquered the small framed mustang he was on. The corral was near the train yard and Josh figured as soon as they got those horses where they could be rode; the horses would be placed on those cattle cars and sent west. Josh and Wija stopped by the corral and sat there watching. The big bay was standing by his self, tied to a post with two ropes, watching the other horses. The army sergeant they had met a day before saw them as they rode up. He had intentions of showing them that the horse could be ridden. He barked out the order for them to bring the bay horse over. Three soldiers went to get him and led him into the corral, kicking and rearing. They tied him to the post in the middle of the corral and after about ten minutes finally got a saddle on him. As one of the soldiers climbed on him Wija sat and smiled. The soldier eased down into the saddle and they let the horse go. The rider lasted all of two seconds before he was in mid air grabbing at anything he could find and yelling. Again and again, rider after rider would climb on and again and again they would end up brushing off their clothes as they would get up off the ground. None of them lasted long enough to figure out which way that horse was going. The sergeant had seen enough and ordered them to hold the horse. He removed his holster and hat then walked towards the horse.

Sergeant Benjamin O'Rourke, a thirty-four year old Irish soldier that had stayed on from the Union Army joining the regular United States Army, just after the Civil War. He was good with horses as far as getting them ready to ride but had no patience for a horse that was head strong. He saw in this horse the same thing that Josh had and even though he didn't like to admit it, he knew Wija was right. He had served in the Union and fought at Shiloh and Gettysburg. He was tough in every sense of the word and felt strange having to supervise confederate soldiers but it was a job and he had earned their respect. With his five feet eleven inch frame and his red wavy hair, he wasn't particularly one that you might fear, but looks were deceiving and he had made his abilities known more than once. At this particular time his Irish temper was coming through. He felt he should be out west fighting Indians and was stuck here because of his last battle fought near Spanish Fort, Alabama at a place called Blakely. If not for that he would be doing what he loved to do, ... fight. Right at this moment he had only one thing on his mind and that was to show Josh and Wija that the horse wasn't all they thought him to be. Sergeant O'Rourke climbed into that saddle and when they let go of that horse, it took just three jumps and O'Rourke hit the ground about as hard as any man can without breaking something. O'Rourke was mad and his face turned redder than his hair.

Wija didn't mean too but he let out a laugh and when he did, that sergeant spun around and headed for his pistol hanging on the fence. He grabbed that gun and as he turned to point it at Wija, Josh drew that Colt and had it dead center on that sergeant's chest. It all happened so fast that not only was Wija shocked but that sergeant and all those soldiers looked like they had swallowed a cat. Josh decided he better get to talking before lead started flying.

"Sir," Josh said, "Now I don't know what you got all riled up about, if it was hitting the ground like that or my friend here laughing. I am going to make a suggestion that you place that pistol back in the holster and we can handle this in another manner. I don't want these fellows here to be carrying your coffin. See Wija here was laughing because he saw what we all saw you thinking you could break that horse even though you have seen your men eat dirt because of him. It may be you just want a fight but I am thinking it is because the horse is as mean as my friend here says and it is going to take something more than just anger to tame him. You will remember me asking you for that horse yesterday and you said no without even giving it any thought. Looks to me that nobody' had any luck with him so far so I would like to propose a deal to you. First you need to lower that pistol and then we can talk." Josh didn't know how mad the sergeant was but he hoped that he didn't have to pull that trigger. He didn't feel good about having to kill a man nor the thought of going to prison.

Sergeant O'Rourke was mad but not mad enough to test Josh's skill with that pistol. He had never seen anyone draw that fast and he sure wasn't about to try him. He nodded to Josh and turned placing the pistol back into the holster. "Okay" he said to Josh, "What's your offer?"

Josh said; "You just got mad at my friend because he was laughing, same as me. Why? Because we have sat here and watched that horse whip nearly ever man you got out here trying to ride him. Wija has told you the horse will not be tamed by anger and even though he may not be the same color as you and I, he does know animals. I would say it wouldn't hurt if you listen to others once in a while they may be able to help you. Now, how many horses do you have left over there to be broke?"

Sergeant O'Rourke said "Maybe ten."

Josh turned to Wija and asked him if he thought they could do it? Wija, nodded yes.

Josh turned to Sergeant O'Rourke and said; "Sir, instead of your troops and you getting all banged up breaking these horses, we will do it for you. Just the ten horses over in that corral. If you accept the offer the only cost will be that big bay. I would like very much to have that horse and breaking them would be my way of paying for your time and trouble of catching him."

Sergeant O'Rourke was a fair man even with his temper. He said; "You have a deal but with one condition, you have to break the bay first." You only have one shot at him and if you fall off, then you still have too break the other horses and the bay stays with us.

Josh got off his horse and was thinking it over. He held his hand out and Sergeant O'Rourke shook it. Josh wanted to make sure that the people gathered saw the deal being made so the sergeant wouldn't go back on his word.

Wija climbed down and started to walk to towards the horse. He was stopped by Sergeant O'Rourke. "Wait, ... first off like I said you have one shot on the bay." "Second," he indicated to Josh, "You have to be the one to break him."

Josh climbed the fence and headed towards the horse. Wija was calming the horse even before Josh got to him while the soldiers walked out of the corral. Josh took his gun belt off and handed it to Wija. Josh was trying to look strong but he wasn't sure if he could ride this horse or not. Josh looked at Wija and asked in a low whisper, what do I need to expect?

Wija grinned and said; "The ride of your life!" "Onile will give you his best and you need to give him yours."

Josh looking wild eyed said; "You mean that is all the advice you can give me? You claim to have talked to this horse and that is all you can say?"

Wija said; "Of course not, sit in the middle, hang on to the reigns, take a deep seat and don't get your self killed."

Josh didn't think it was that funny and after getting into the saddle was fixing to express his concerns when Wija said; "Remember your maw needs you." He then let the rope go.

It seemed an eternity, that bay horse kicking and bucking. He grunted and slobbered doing everything in his power to get Josh out of the saddle. Josh hung on as if he was a tick on a dog's back. The horse would spin one way then the other and Josh would adjust. Josh was beginning to fade and could just picture having to break all those horses while losing the chance to get Onile. Every time he would feel himself slipping, he would grab another hold with his spurs and dig in. All of a sudden Onile started easing up and then stopped bucking. It was finished and Josh now had the horse he wanted. Onile began to walk and Josh immediately felt the horse relax under him. Even though it would still take time, trust would be built and a friendship started.

"I'll just be damned," Sergeant O'Rourke said. "Well a deal is a deal." He walked up to Josh and lifted his hand. "You are quiet a salty fellow for being so young. I have seen you draw a gun, ride, stand your ground and take up for those you consider friends, anything else I need to know about you?"

Josh said; "Sergeant my name is Josh Wilkes and if I like you I will be loyal to you. A friendship is hard to come by no matter what color the skin, where a person comes from or what they have done in the past. Friendship is something to hold on too."

"Well you would have been good in the war. You have earned my respect and I am glad to know you. My name is Benjamin O'Rourke, my friends call me Ben." Josh took his hand and thanked him. "Before we get all friendly now, there are still those horses over there that need to be broke. We will be shipping them out in a couple of days. If you need me just give me a yell."

Wija and Josh went to work breaking the remaining horses and it was almost dark before they finished keeping their part of the bargain. When they finished they were tired and sore. They each climbed on their horse and headed home with Onile in tow. He was a beauty but at this particular time neither of the young men cared about riding him. A hot tub of water and a good soaking, some food and a night's rest was what was needed. As they headed for the ranch, Josh couldn't help but think of Christine and it was strange but he felt the need to be near her just as he knew he wanted Onile. Of course there was a big difference in the woman and the horse, but he hadn't figured out any way to get her attention yet. It was something to ponder on but as for now there were many other things that needed tending too. The moon was up by the time they reached the ranch and Alicia was standing on the porch waiting on them. Hearing the story of what had happened in town, she was pleased that they were safe. After their bath, both of them ate and quickly retired to bed. Tomorrow would be a new day and Josh would be able to start working with Onile. The crickets chirped as he put his head on the pillow. He thought about the horse and the girl, and quickly fell asleep. In what seemed like no time the rooster crowed.

Chapter 3

LEARNING TO TRUST

Josh completed all the chores he had to do within a few hours and turned his attention to the horse. Tim and Wija joined him as they all began to show Onile that he was safe. Tim had a wealth of knowledge when it came to horses and he knew right away that this horse was special. The horse was smart and picked up on things real quick. A little feisty when Josh first climbed on him, he settled down quickly. He figured out what Josh wanted and within a few hours he was acting as if he had been doing this stuff all along. Tim and Wija saddled up and all three went out to check the ranch and see if there had been anymore cattle missing. In riding out into the open, it would be the first time that Onile had been so close to freedom since his capture. How he would react was a question that Josh wanted answered! As they rode out of the corral, Onile's head and ears picked up but he stayed at a walk. Josh could feel the power of the horse and knew if the horse wanted to be free, there would be nothing he could do. After about a mile from the barn, Onile relaxed and it was then that Josh felt at ease.

They rode the fence line and didn't find anymore signs of broken fences. Cattle were scattered so there was no way to be sure if anymore cattle were missing especially with as many head as was on the ranch. Yet something was wrong and Josh couldn't put his finger on it. Wija was feeling uneasy too and made the statement that he had a bad feeling about the day. Tim told the boys to be aware of everything and keep their eyes open. Old Tim had been feeling uneasy since the cattle went missing but he wasn't about to let them know it. Those cattle missing were strange because they hadn't lost any since the war had ended. It wasn't uncommon for the union or confederate soldiers to come in and take some cattle to help feed their troops but even then you would know that they were going too. They would always promise to make sure that the Wilkes was compensated but no money ever came from either army. Today was pleasant for the three and Old Tim, if he could, wanted to make sure that it stayed that way.

Tim was thinking about the ranch and wondering if everything would ever settle down where he and other colored people would be able to walk around with their head up. He was glad to be with the Wilkes and even though he didn't know that much about Mr. Wilkes, Edonta had told him of the kind of man he was and how he treated all folks. Tim would like to meet him and if Mrs. Alicia's feeling of Mr. Wilkes returning was right, then he would get the chance. If Mr. Wilkes didn't come home then it would be hard on her and Josh to keep things going but Tim was determined to help them with everything he could. Tim had already heard about the incident in town and how quick Josh was with the gun. It didn't bother him about what Josh did because he had been around long enough to watch Josh mature as a man. Josh was level headed and from what he could hear, handled himself pretty good with that sergeant. When all was said and done Tim would be there to help the Wilkes because he had been taken in even though he was a stranger. He was tended too and nurse back to health by people he didn't know and he was beholding to them. He would give his life for the Wilkes if he had too.

The sun was dropping to the horizon when the three started back. They were on the road that runs between the Ruffkin Plantation and Wilkes farm. About a quarter mile ahead of them they saw a wagon with two people on it. With the daylight dimming quick, they couldn't tell who it was but all of a sudden the man driving the wagon fell off and the two horses bolted. The passenger fell back into the cargo area and there was no one in control. Josh yelled at Wija and Tim to check on the driver and he hit Onile with the spurs. It was then that Josh found out the power of the horse. Josh could feel the horse move out and his jump was so quick that Josh just sat back feeling the power of the horse push him deep into the saddle. It was as though Onile knew what he was supposed to do. Even though the wagon was a good ways ahead of them, Onile was galloping at a pace such as Josh had never experienced before. Josh watched the wagon as it got closer and closer. Onile's run was nearing three quarters

never seen one that moved as fast as Onile. He will not be beat."

They all rambled on about the speed at which Onile moved. Josh and Wija listened to Tim as he told of the many horses he had seen run. Tim knew this horse was special from the first time he saw him. After watching him run, there was no doubt about his spirit and Tim had the feeling he was destined to be great.

After breakfast the next morning, Tim and Josh started working with Onile. The horse would respond to their request and it wasn't long before Tim had him doing things that Josh never thought possible. Wija joined them and all three worked the horse with only Josh and Wija riding him. Tim told them that Onile would not allow anyone on his back but those he trusted and at this time that would only be them. He also began to work with Onile on coming to Josh when he was summoned. Tim would let Onile wonder off then whistle and clap his hands once. He then had Josh repeat it every time Onile would walk away and not be paying attention. Onile would look back at Josh but he didn't seem to pay much attention, sometimes coming and sometimes not. After a full day of working with the horse, Tim headed to take care of his chores with Wija. Josh brushed Onile down and set him loose in the paddock. He closed the gate and turned to watch Onile as he nuzzled a horse across the fence. He remembered the words that Wija had spoke when he first saw Onile, "He will not be tamed by anger." It seemed true as he had seen the horse change and now start to trust them. Josh whistled and clapped his hands. Onile turned and looked at him then went back to the horse across the fence. Josh smiled and thought to himself, maybe he just needs a little more trust.

As he approached the house, Josh saw a horse tied to the rail out front. As he entered he saw Mr. Ruffkin sitting on the sofa speaking to his mom. He greeted him and was fixing to go to his room when Ruffkin stood and extended his hand. Josh shook his hand as Ruffkin thanked him for helping his niece. Ruffkin then excused himself and left but Josh knew he was there for something else and asked his mom what the man wanted. She was quiet for a minute but then looked at Josh and said he wants our place. Josh was irate, he was mad as a hen and started stomping and cursing, something he never did in front of his mother.

"Why?" asked Josh, "Doesn't he have enough land already?" "He owns half the county, the lumber yard and shipping company by the river." Why does he want our land?"

Alicia told Josh to calm down because she had no intentions of selling the land to anyone. She said that Ruffkin explained that he wanted to build another wharf on the river to send cotton and lumber down to Mobile. He felt that Josh and she could use the money and start a new life away from the bad memories of being where her husband once lived and worked. She told Ruffkin she would not do anything without her husband's approval. She felt Mr. Ruffkin became upset with her notion that Jonathan would return and was going to chastise her but that was when Josh came in so he didn't say anything.

Josh asked her what he offered. Land at the time was selling for nine dollars and twenty cents an acre and his mom said that Ruffkin offered them ten dollars and acre. That was about eighty cents an acre over the cost. In all he offered them eight thousand one hundred and twenty dollars. This was suspicious to Josh and he wondered why the man would offer almost eighty cents an acre more than it was worth. Why did a man who owned so much land want more farm land? There was something wrong, Josh couldn't put his finger on it just yet but he was sure going to be watching. He felt a little better after super but went to bed thinking and asking himself why? Ruffkin had other ideas and Josh was sure that sooner or later it would come out. He just didn't like the thought of it messing up his chances at getting to see Christine. As he closed his eyes he could see her and soon went off to sleep with pleasant thought of her on his mind.

Chapter 4

TROUBLES ON THE RANCH

Alicia and Zuri were cooking breakfast when they could hear the sound of several gun shots. They walked out into the back yard and heard several more then saw smoke coming from the direction of an old line shack that was a couple of miles from the house. Josh was getting ready when the sound of the shots caught his attention. He quickly went outside where he met Wija and Edonta. They began to talk when Enu ran up and said Tim was gone.

"Gone where?" Edonta asked.

Enu said, "He said to tell you he was going to check the fences and would be back later." He went early this morning and he rode off in the direction those shots are coming from. Enu looked worried as did Edonta. Alicia told Josh and Wija to go and see if they could find Tim. She then looked at Josh and told him to be careful. Josh promised her they would be okay and went to the barn to get the horses.

Wija had already saddled Onile and another horse and they quickly left the barn towards the old line shack. About a quarter of mile from the shack, Josh and Wija split up. Josh got off of Onile about two hundred yards from the shack in the woods and walked the rest of the way on foot so as to keep his presence unknown in case anyone was there. The shots had stopped but Josh knew now that what ever was happening was happening on their property. As he neared an opening to the shack, he could see that it was on fire and he saw three men on horses near two dead cows. The men had black hoods over their heads, covering their faces. All of them were armed. The smoke from the fire was rising through the trees. There was an opening of about seventy yards from the wood line to the house and Josh didn't want to confront the men that far from cover so he worked his way around the woods to get closer. He was about twenty yards from the men, and was fixing to step out when he saw two more riders coming from the back side of the shack. They too had hoods over their heads and something else, Tim, with a rope around him. He was walking ahead of their horses and they both had guns pointing at him.

Tim was bleeding from the mouth and looked to have been roughed up. It wasn't a secret that when they reached the other three, they intended on hurting Tim or worse killing him. They were all admiring their handy work with the shack and cows they had killed but now they were talking about Tim and what they would do with him. The biggest one of them made reference to Tim as being protected by the Wilkes and that they should string him up so as to make an example to other colored folks in the area. A shorter man said he would have nothing to do with it because they had their orders and the boss wouldn't like it if they didn't do as they were told. Josh was hoping for a name but didn't get one.

Yeah the big guy said, "We ain't supposed to harm anyone of the Wilkes but the boss didn't say anything about coloreds." The shorter man re-stated his position and turned and rode off. The other three men stayed and after some discussion, they decided to hang Tim. They drug him to a big oak near the shack and threw the end of the rope over a limb. One of the riders got off his horse and took the rope from around Tim's waist and moved it up around his neck. After wrapping the rope around the saddle horn a rider rode forward taking the slack out of the rope until Tim was standing on his toes with his hands tied behind him.

The four men never saw Josh as he stepped out of the woods behind them. Just as Tim's feet left the ground a shot rang out and the rope that had stretched tight was cut in too, dropping Tim back to the ground. With accuracy, Josh had cut the rope with his bullet and now had his colt trained on the men. None of them moved nor spoke so Josh started the conversation.

"You fellows," Josh said; "Are looking for trouble and it is my guess you have found it. You are trespassing on our property and old Tim here works for us. It really aggravates me since this is the second time this week that I have had to pull this gun and so far I haven't done what I was taught to do with it." None of the riders were moving a muscle but one did muster up enough courage to ask Josh what he meant.

Josh exclaimed, "My paw told me to never pull this gun unless I intended to use it. The other day I pulled the gun and it along with some conversation worked, but today I feel that one or all of you want to try me and I may just have to act as my paw taught me and kill somebody."

The big man asked; "You Josh Wilkes?"

"That would be me," Josh said.

"Well," the big man said; "You have just bought yourself a peck of misery. We don't want you or the coloreds around here and we aim to see that all of you move out of here. You don't know who you're messing with kid."

Josh was beginning to anger and he knew at this time he needed to keep a level head. "Well mister, I am figuring that at this point and time, I have the gun on you and I am the one who figures to deal with this problem. Now the way I see this, you all have already stole some cattle, killed some cattle and set fire to property belonging to us. Not to mention you tried to hang this man. Josh cut Tim's hands loose and told him to go fetch the horses. I ain't real sure if I am going to just kill all of you or take you to Sheriff Dunkin. Josh knew he couldn't watch all four of them and figured his best chance was to disarm them and get those hoods off."

None of these fellows acted ready to try Josh but he was reading their body language pretty good even though he couldn't see their faces. Josh figured the two on the left didn't want a fight, one was shaking and the other hadn't taken his hands down. The big man was calm and showed it in his voice. He wore his gun low on the right side and Josh felt he would know how to use it. It had a pearl handle and if Josh was a betting man, he would say this fellow was a hired gunman. The other fellow was fidgety and would probably make the first move. What the big man didn't realize was that Josh was using him as a shield. Josh even knew when this man was going to react. His gun was higher on his hip and he would be the first Josh would have to deal with. The big man's gun was lower and in the sitting position, he would have a little harder time getting to it. Josh's only hope was that the other two fellows wouldn't get involved. No sense in putting it off now was the time and Josh meant to be ready for whatever happened.

Josh spoke; "We are going to Sheriff Dunkin so what I need for you fellows to do is unbuckle those guns and drop them to the ground then you will remove the hoods." Just as Josh had figured, the fidgety man spun his horse to the side and drew his gun. The bigger man was grabbing his gun at the same time. Josh fired one shot; shooting the gun out of the first mans hand and quickly turned his attention to the big man. The big fellow had done this before and had already cleared his holster, drawing a bead on Josh. All of a sudden the pearl handled gun came out of the big mans hand and fell to the ground. He grabbed at the knife that had struck him in the shoulder and winced in pain. All four of the riders took off riding hard and in the direction of the Ruffkin plantation. Josh had the feeling that they were not just passing across Ruffkin's land.

Wija walked up from behind the tree that he had been standing behind. Josh asked him where he learned to use a knife like that and he said, Tim. At that time Tim was walking out of the woods with his horse and Onile. Wija leaned over and picked up the pearl handled pistol. He looked it over and started to hand it to Josh.

Josh said; "It's yours, keep it."

Wija said; "Well I guess I could and trade him when we run into them again."

Josh asked; "Trade for what?"

"My knife," Wija replied, "That was my best knife, maybe he will give it back to me."

"Yeah," said Josh; "That would be something, by the way thanks for the help but I think I had it under control."

Wija said; 'Maybe so and maybe not, could be that I just didn't want to miss out on the fun, either way I saved your bacon as usual."

Josh acted surprised, "You saved my bacon, wait a minute, you had a knife, they had guns, think about that before you start getting medals." Deep inside though Josh knew that Wija had probably saved his life.

They didn't trail the riders but instead, cleaned up the mess they had made and stayed to make sure the fire didn't spread to the woods. It was getting late before they started back home. Tim had already left to let Mrs. Wilkes know what had happened and that they were safe. Josh knew they would run into those men again. It wouldn't be hard to find them but the next time the outcome would probably be worse.

As they neared the house Josh saw Mr. Ruffkins horse again tied up in front. Josh brushed and fed Onile and cut him loose. The horse ran off kicking and bucking before settling down and munching on grass. Josh whistled and clapped his hands and Onile just looked up at him. Again Josh figured that the horse was just being stubborn and hadn't learned how to trust him all the way. Josh headed towards the house with Wija. Ruffkins was standing in the living room and both Josh and Wija acknowledged him, neither of them saying anything. Mrs. Wilkes told them she was glad they were safe and asked if they had found out who the men were. Ruffkin looked at them and had no emotions on his face as Josh began to explain the events that occurred.

"There were five of them, all hooded. They set fire to the line shack and killed a couple of cows then they decided they was fixing to stretch Old Tim's' neck. Probably would have if Wija and I hadn't of come along." Josh figured his mom already knew but he wanted Ruffkin to hear it. Ruffkin stood up and tried to act concerned but Josh wasn't buying it.

"You don't know who they were Ruffkin asked?" "No," Josh replied, "But we should be able to find them pretty easy. I hit one of them in the hand and Wija got a blade in the other one. They took off, heading in the direction of your place." Ruffkin headed for the door and said he needed to get to his place to make sure they weren't around.

Wija couldn't hold his tongue anymore. "Mr. Ruffkin, if you don't mind, tells the big fellow to save my knife, I sure would like to get it back."

Ruffkin stopped and glared at Wija and it was obvious that he would have shot him if he could have got away with it. "I don't like your insinuations; you don't know who you are messing with." Wija was fixing to reply but Josh grabbed his arm and said, "I will handle this."

Josh looked at Ruffkin and said; "You know sir, it is strange, we have lost a dozen cattle a couple a days ago. Today we had some more killed for no reason and a line shack burned to the ground. What I find curious is that those yahoo's came across your land to get on ours and that you know nothing about it. It is also strange that nothing of yours has been messed with and this afternoon they made threats to run us off our land, land that you Mr. Ruffkin for some reason, have all of a sudden became interested in." Ruffkin didn't want to interrupt and he didn't want to stand there and listen either but this was one time he had no choice.

Josh continued; "I don't know if those men work for you, if they do it will come to light. What I do know is that twice today I have been told that I didn't know who I was messing with." Well Ruffkin, I really don't care, see "I will do what I need too, to protect this ranch and the families that live here until my paw comes home." "So sir," "If you happen to run into those fellows you can tell them for me, they don't know who they are messing with. All that said you may want to pay attention to who is on your land, good night Mr. Ruffkin."

Ruffkin made no comment and left the house with the front screen door slamming behind him. Mrs. Wilkes looked at Josh in awe and said "Y'all wash up for supper."

Chapter 5

COMING TOGETHER

ALICIA HAD GONE to Jackson and reported the incident at the line shack to Sheriff Dunkin. She didn't want Josh or Wija to go just in case the men were there. It had now been several days since anything had happened. No one traveled alone from the ranch for safety reasons. There was plenty to do and everyone stayed busy. It gave Josh a lot of time to work with Onile and ride him around, getting to know his habits. The horse was aware of everything that went on and even though he still wouldn't come when Josh whistled and clapped his hand, the horse was forming a partnership and trust.

Josh had ridden out to check the north side of the property, checking fences and looking for anything suspicious. As he neared the Ruffkin Plantation, he saw Christine riding up the road on a paint mare. She waved at him and he started riding in her direction. They met and stopped to talk for a moment which turned into an afternoon. Both of them asked questions about each other and ended up near a small lake close to a limestone company just off both of their properties. It was August and very hot. The lake water cooled the air some and they found a shade tree and sat in the grass after letting the horses drink.

Christine began to talk of her uncle and said she didn't understand a lot of the things he did or why he did them. It was apparent that she was appreciative of him taking her in and caring for her but she also was knew he was not being honest about everything he had done. Josh asked her about the men he had encountered at the line shack. To his and her surprise, she had not heard of the events that had taken place.

"What happened?" asked Christine.

Josh explained the events and that her uncle was at his home when he got there. He then asked her had she seen any new faces around the plantation.

Christine told him there were three men that she did not like. They had come to the plantation about a month ago to work for her uncle. She had heard that they came from a place called Rag Swamp near Mobile and were wanted for robbery and murder. She didn't know if it was true but the biggest one gave her the creeps. One of the men called him James but she didn't know anything else about him or the other two. She also told Josh that one of them had his hand wrapped because he had gotten it caught in some barbwire.

Christine was thinking about why her Uncle Clarence hadn't said anything to her about the trouble that had occurred. He was protective of her in a weird kind of way and even though he was kinfolk, she didn't approve of how he ran the plantation or the people that worked for him. Not telling her about the trouble at the Wilkes ranch even had her wondering what was going on. As for now though she was watching Josh and was feeling that some girl would be lucky to get a rope on him. He was handsome and strong looking and had a way of carrying himself that people around talked about especially the young ladies.

Josh had listened and now he knew without a doubt that Ruffkin was in some way connected to the men but he wanted to be sure. If they just happened to be working there and using his place as a hideout, Josh didn't want to make a false accusation that would cause him any problems with Christine. He sat and looked at her beauty and wanted desperately to tell her how he felt. He didn't think Ruffkin would like it though and was keeping his feeling to himself. Christine reached over and took him by the hand. He felt like a school kid, kicking dirt but he knew those days were long gone and his feeling meant much more now that he was older.

They talked for over an hour and Josh noticed some storm clouds coming up on the horizon. They both agreed that it may be time to head home and stood up. Josh helped Christine to her feet and she stumbled forward landing against his chest. She looked up into Josh's eyes and they kissed. It wasn't a long kiss but it was enough for both of them to know that they wanted more. Josh helped her onto the horse and she looked at him. She took his hand and said; "I'll be seeing you again Joshua Wilkes."

"Do you like me?" Josh asked.

"Yes I like you," Christine replied, "I like you a lot." She smiled and rode off. Josh was sure glad because he had turned red but he already knew he didn't want it to be too long before he saw her again. Lightning flashed in the distance and Josh climbed on Onile and headed back towards the ranch house.

The wind picked up and it began to rain, first just a mist and a change from the hot muggy air to the coolness with the approaching rain. The trees started to sway back and forth then the rain drops got as big as half dollars. Josh put his poncho on and kept his head down and was hoping that Christine got home okay. He was still three or four miles from the house and the clouds had turned dark enough that it appeared like night had set in. Onile kept his head down as the rain pelted Josh and him. Josh decided that he would find some shelter and wait for the storm to pass.

It was mid July to early August when these storms would pop up in the afternoon. His paw had told him it was the time of the years known as "dog days." He still wasn't sure what a dog had to do with it but his paw told him it had something to do with a dog star in the sky called Sirius that helped the sun add heat making the days the hottest of the year. He really didn't care that much about it but knew that it was hot and these strong storms were dangerous with all the lightning and hail that would come from them. Josh was looking for anything to get out of the weather when there was a bolt of lightning that struck a tree limb above him. Onile spun as the huge oak limb fell and struck Josh in the head and shoulder, knocking him to the ground. Josh struggled to get up but was dazed and didn't know where Onile had gone. The rain was pounding him and he could see blood on the rain soaked ground. He lifted his hand and felt a large lump and cut on the back of his head. Josh grabbed his hat and again tried to get up but fell back to the ground. He could feel himself losing consciousness and was fighting to stay awake.

He could not get up and decided to lie still when he felt a shove on his back. Onile was pushing him with his nose. Onile stepped up beside Josh as if he was waiting on him to get back on. Josh grabbed the stirrup and pulled himself up to a sitting position. He sat there a few minutes and again pulled himself up by using the saddle. He didn't know if he could climb on and began talking to the horse. "I don't think I can make it;" Josh said. "You are just too tall for me." As if he knew what Josh was saying, Onile stretched out until Josh was able to fall over the saddle and right himself. Onile stood up and began walking with the rain still pelting them. The lighting and wind was the hardest Josh could remember but he couldn't worry about it, he had to hang on and find shelter. He saw a bunch of trees that may help knock the rain off but he didn't have the strength to get Onile to go that way. Josh slumped in the saddle and he lost consciousness. It seemed but a few seconds and he came around enough to see that Onile had walked into a cavern. It was now dark and he couldn't see anything but the lightning that was flashing outside the entrance. Cold and wet he eased off of Onile and lay on the ground. He reached up and loosened the girth on the saddle and passed out again.

Josh awoke with Onile nuzzling him with his nose. He had been out for several hours and could not see anything but a dim light at the opening of the cavern. He remembered getting off the horse but not how Onile got them there. His head felt as if there were drums being pounded in it. He took things slow and it took him a minute to stand. He tightened the saddle on Onile the best he could and struggled but managed to get back on the horse. The blood had dried on his shirt and the cut on his head was still bleeding but had almost stopped. Onile walked out of the cavern and down a slope, through some bushes and into an open area around thirty yards wide and fifty yards long. It was flat and just to one side of it was the river. The cavern was concealed by the trees and brush. The night sky was full of stars as all the storm clouds had gone. A half moon was just rising over the trees and Josh figured it was late, close to midnight or after. He slumped over in the saddle and let Onile walk, hoping that he would find his way home.

Alicia was in a panic. She had sent Wija and Edonta out towards the river. Tim and Enu went towards the Ruffkin Plantation. The storm had hit fast and caused a twister that tore through the property blowing trees over. No one had got hurt and the house was fine but Alicia was concerned that Josh was injured. She was standing on the porch when Tim and Enu returned along with Christine. She had made it back to the plantation but she knew Josh didn't have time to make it home. She left the plantation as soon as the storm ended and was headed towards the Wilkes home when she met up with Tim and Enu. She showed them where she left Josh and even though Tim was a good tracker the rain had washed out any tracks that might have been left.

Wija and Edonta rode the river but when it got dark they couldn't see anymore and decided to return to the ranch and wait till daylight. Wija knew Josh could take care of himself but it didn't cause him not to worry. Josh was like his brother and he couldn't imagine what would happen to the ranch if something happened to him. They made it back and it was obvious that there was concern. Alicia Wilkes was a strong woman but not knowing was the worst. She didn't know where Jonathan was or if he would ever come home. She would not be able to make it without Josh. She looked up into the night sky asking God to let Josh be okay and to bring him home. Nobody was asleep, nobody wanted to sleep. Zuri brought coffee to the living room and they all sit in silence. It was quiet and no one saying anything until Enu said; "Listen, I hear something." No one else could hear it but Enu said; "There is a horse coming." Again they all listened and herd the snort of a horse. Wija ran out the front door and yelled at the others, "It is Josh, he is hurt, come quickly." Edonta and Wija helped Josh down and carried him into the house. Alicia looked into the night sky and said; 'Thank you."

When dawn broke Edonta went to get Doc Taylor from Jackson. He was the only doctor and veterinarian in two counties. He also did some blacksmith work and was good at all three. He had been a doctor in the war and had returned home after the surrender of Lee to Grant. He traveled a lot and it was unsure if he would be at his home or in Mount Vernon.

Josh was pretty much sleeping all the time and everyone took turns sitting with him. His mom had got the bleeding to stop with a mixture of herbs that Zuri had put together. The cut would heal with time but Josh couldn't seem to stay awake. He would arouse but never talk and as fast as he woke up he would go back to sleep and that concerned everybody.

Christine refused to go back to the plantation and was catching cat naps on the sofa when she could. She would sit with Josh while the others rested. Her uncle had sent a worker looking for her and she told him that she would be at the Wilkes farm until Josh got better. Wija was silent and his face showed the concern he had for his friend.

One thing Wija knew for sure was that Onile had saved Josh's life. When Wija unsaddled Onile he could tell the horse was different. It was as if the horse knew that something was wrong with Josh. Wija walked Onile towards the barn and noticed that the horse kept looking back towards the house. Wija had told everyone that the horse was a protector and he would take care of his herd. In Josh's case, Onile was protecting a companion that he had come to trust in a very short time. Onile knew that Josh was in trouble and he had helped Josh in every way that he could. Some how Onile figured out he had to get Josh home and he did. Wija brushed Onile down, fed him then turned him out into the paddock. Onile didn't eat much and when he got out where he could run, he didn't. He walked down the fence until he could see the front of the house. He stood there, not taking his eyes off of the house. He was waiting on Josh.

Doc Taylor came back with Edonta and tended to Josh. He left instructions for them to clean the wound everyday and keep his head bandaged. I feel like he will be just fine Doc Taylor told Alicia. It is a mighty bad lump but it's a long way from his heart. He is a strong young man, he will be fine. After eating supper, Doc headed down towards Mount Vernon. He had some folks to check on and he would stop back by on his way home.

Wija walked with Doc Taylor too his carriage. "Doc, if you don't mind me asking," Wija said; "Have you doctored any strangers in Jackson lately?" Doc thought and said; "Yeah, two men came in at the same time. One of em said he had been cut by barbwire. That ain't what it looked like to me though. The other one was a big man and had a wound to his shoulder. He told me it was a machete but I know a knife wound when I see it and barbwire don't mess up a hand like that either."

Wija told the doctor about the meeting Josh and he had with the four men at the shack. Sounds to me from what you have described, the two I fixed up are the two fellows you had the run in with. I want to tell you something Doc said; "You and Josh need to be careful." Those two men were escorted to my office by Sheriff Dunkin. I don't know what they are doing around here but my gut tells me they are up to no good. I asked around and found out a little about them. The big man is called James. I have been told that he was the head man in a gang of outlaws from down around Mobile. They are supposed to be wanted in Louisiana, Mississippi and Alabama for everything from robbing banks, steeling cattle and murder. I would guess the men you saw with him are a part of that bunch. This one called James, I feel like he would kill you for spitting on the ground and then sit down and eat a steak while your corpse lay on the floor. If they are the ones y'all met up with, you two need to be watchful because they are mean.

"We will Doc" Wija assured him, "Thank you for coming." There was no question that Doc had worked on the two men from the shack. What was puzzling Wija was that Sheriff Dunkin apparently knew them? It would be a question that needed answering. If they knew Sheriff Dunkin and was working at the Ruffkin place something was sure to be going on. If the sheriff and Ruffkin were working together things could get worse. It was something to ponder over and Wija would be glad when Josh got better.

Josh opened his eyes and knew he was in his own bedroom. What he didn't know was how he got there or how long. He remembered the storm, the rain and lightening flashing. He remembered the tree limb falling on him but that was about it. Realizing that someone was holding his hand, he looked to his left. Christine had her head down on the edge of the bed and was asleep. It was dark outside the window and he could hear the night sounds, crickets chirping, frog croaking and a whip o whil off near the river. A gentle and comforting breeze was rustling the curtains. He squeezed Christine's hand and she lifted her head and looked up.

"Hey," Josh said; "Christine sat up and smiled, hey to you she said."

Josh first questions were how is Onile and how long have I been here? Christine assured him that Onile was fine and then told him he had been asleep for almost three days. Onile got you home, how we don't know but he did.

Josh thought and said I remember some now, I thought when I got knocked off by the limb that he had ran off but he didn't. He stood next to me so that I could pull myself into the saddle. He lowered his body to make it easier for me as if he knew I was having problems. He then got us out of the weather. Josh tried to sit up but was still a little weak. Christine stopped him just as Alicia walked into the room. Alicia walked over and hugged him. "We are so glad you are back with us son." Josh said; "Mom I wasn't gone anywhere, I was just finding a way to keep you from working me so hard." They all laughed.

Christine stood up and said that she needed to get home before her uncle disowned her. Alicia left the room to get Josh some soup. "I am glad you are here" Josh said, "It was great seeing you when I opened my eyes." "It is what it is," replied Christine, "You needed me and I needed to be here for you."

Josh in a shy manner said, "I would hate to lose you especially since I just found you." Christine looked at him, "You are not going to lose me, just get better and we can plan a future together." She leaned over and kissed him, this time it was different, soft and personal, and then she said "I think we are good together." Josh nodded in agreement "I think you are on to something."

Chapter 6

TROUBLES A PLENTY

The morning light came through the window and Josh felt good. He had been up a while and for the first morning was moving around without being light headed or dizzy. Doc Taylor had came by and checked on him and just warned him to take it easy a few more days. Well Josh was ready to start doing things. He had been cramped up for several days and wanted to get outside. Wija and Tim had been working Onile but they had both said he wasn't acting right. He was off of his feed and was cantankerous. He had walked a rut up and down the fence line and would not go with the other horses into the meadow. He stayed to where he could see the house.

Ruffkin had paid another visit to Mrs. Wilkes and spoke to her about the ranch. Again she told him no. Tim had been keeping a watch on the cattle and had reported more missing. It seemed as though they were being taken just a few at a time. Some wires on a fence post had been

cut and wrapped around the post. Tim said that whoever was taking the cattle tried to make it look like the fence was fine but when you pulled on the wire it would come off the post. Once they got the cattle they wanted they would just put the wire back so no one would notice.

Wija had told Josh of the conversation with Doc Taylor. It made Josh wonder who he could trust but his biggest concern was why Ruffkin wanted the ranch. There were a lot of questions but Josh knew there would be answers and the sooner the better.

Of course his most pleasant thoughts were about Christine. When she was near he didn't worry about anything. He enjoyed her company and pictured her and him sitting on a porch drinking coffee and planning out their day. He didn't know if it would happen but it was a dream he lived over and over.

After breakfast Josh walked out onto the porch. It was good to be outside and smell the fresh morning air. It hadn't got hot yet but by noon the sun would be beaming down and everyone would be looking for a shade. Sweat came easy in late August and the temperature stayed hot even in the evenings. Josh stepped off of the porch and looked towards the corral. Onile was standing there looking at him. The second that Onile saw Josh the horse began to prance and his ears went up. Onile strutted, throwing his head, kicking, bucking and whinnying. He would run with his tail up showing everyone that he was in charge. It was obvious he was glad to see Josh.

Tim ran from the barn to see what all the commotion was about and when he saw Josh he just started laughing. You are his partner Josh. He has been waiting on you.

Onile calmed down and headed for a pile of hay. His appetite had returned but he didn't take his eyes off of Josh. Josh walked to the fence, whistled and clapped his hands. Onile lifted his head and looked then turned his rear towards Josh and went back to eating. Josh just shook his head and smiled to himself as he walked towards the barn. Tim met him and welcomed him back to the world. He then told Josh that more cattle had went missing. He expected probably thirty or more. It wasn't that Tim really knew because he couldn't read or write, Wija told him. Wija had learned a lot from Mrs. Wilkes and had enough education to get by on. Tim just felt good acting like he knew.

I am going to Jackson tomorrow and talk with Sheriff Dunkin. I don't know what his dealings with those men are but I would like to feel him out and see how he reacts. Tim warned Josh to be careful. Those men got a mean streak in em and they don't mind hurting anyone. You done got the jump on em once, you my not be so lucky this time. Josh assured him he would be very careful. You take care of things around here Josh told Tim and I will take Wija with me. They talked a spell about Onile as they walked back to the fence. Onile came walking up and Josh began rubbing his neck and talking to him. Onile never moved as Josh spoke as if he was listening to every thing that was said. A bond had formed between the two and they both knew they would take care of each other.

On the way to Jackson, Josh and Wija stopped at the stockyard in Leroy. Josh wanted to see if there had been any strangers bringing cattle in to sell and more so if those cattle had the Wilkes Bar brand on them. Josh didn't figure that cattle stolen from the ranch would be sold so close to the ranch especially with the ranch brand on them. The only other stockyard was in Mobile and that was three days ride. They looked through the yard at some of the cattle but didn't spot any of theirs. The owner of the stockyard said he would keep his eyes open and check with the owner from Mobile to see if he had purchased any with the Josh's family brand. It was felt that he would since Josh's dad had always brought his cattle there to sell.

As they got near Fort Colman Josh saw Sergeant O'Rourke. The soldiers with him were working with some new horses, training them to work while riding in formations. It was good to have the horses riding next to each other and was a common practice with the cavalry. No one wanted to ride next to a horse that was acting up and causing a stir with the other horses. Sergeant O'Rourke was giving orders and teaching the soldiers as well as the horses how to prepare themselves for what ever they came up against. They looked disciplined but Josh had no urges to join them. Sergeant O'Rourke waved and then turned the squad over to his corporal. He rode over to Josh and Wija.

"Hey fellows," O'Rourke said; "How have ya been?" Before Josh could answer he said "I hear you were in a bad way for a spell?"

"Yeah," said Josh; "Got bummed up during the storm but I am feeling a lot better."

Sergeant O'Rourke looked over at the big bay horse and asked how he was working out?

Josh told him that Onile was doing fine. If not for him I would have been a lot worse off.

O'Rourke then asked them if they had been having any problems at the ranch.

"Yeah," Josh said; "Why do you ask?"

Well we get into town on weekends O'Rourke said. "There has been some talk about it. People are saying that y'all are losing cattle and stuff. A runt of a fellow says you and Wija will be having some problems because you messed up a couple of men on your place. They aim to make things tuff on your ma and you. There intentions are to get you off your land from what I hear."

"Do you know who they are or who brought them in to do this?" asked Josh.

"No I didn't hear any names mentioned but we were at the saloon and the runt was pretty drunk," replied O'Rourke. "I do know that he works for Ruffkin." "You and Wija need to watch your back and if I hear anything else, I will surely let you know. We will be keeping an ear to the ground about any cattle being stolen too. We have the authority to act on a rustler if we catch em. If you need us, just let me know."

"Oh, by the way, you two interested in parlaying for another horse?" "I have about fifteen that needs to be broke before I can ship them off."

Josh looked at Sergeant O'Rourke as if he had a bump on his head. "I sure ain't and I don't believe Wija is either. It took us a couple of days to get over the soreness of breaking them other ones." Wija just sit and nodded in agreement.

Sergeant O'Rourke left them with a warning to be careful and rode off to catch up with his troops.

No one was at Sheriff Dunkins office and the only thing you could hear in the town was the sound of the piano from the saloon. It was hot and Saturday. Things were sure to pick up around dark.

Josh went into the bank and spoke to Mr. McIntosh, the bank president. He checked on the land taxes owed and found that they would be short on the taxes by about seven hundred dollars. It was a problem but nothing that couldn't be handled. First he needed to find out who was steeling the cattle.

Wija was waiting near the horses when he saw a man go into the saloon. He had a wrapped right hand and kept looking at Wija. Josh came out of the bank and when the man seen him, went into the saloon at a pretty fast pace. Wija told Josh about him but Josh knew that he would not be in any shape to challenge the man. He still needed a few more days to get his mind straight and be able to control things.

They walked over to the general store to buy some supplies. Just as they reached the door Josh spotted an announcement tacked to the wall. It appeared there was going to be a stake race for any rider that had a horse they wanted to enter. The only catch was the cost to enter was one hundred dollars with the winner getting one thousand dollars. The course was from the middle of town to a big oak about a half mile outside of town and back. The race involved two riders with one horse. Once the first rider reached the big oak, he would turn the horse over to the second rider that would complete the race. It was a pretty good distance but Josh felt that Onile could make the run easily. After all he had been chased by the soldiers for several months before they caught him. The race was to be the first Saturday in September at the yearly town gathering. It was kind of like a county fair. That would mean they would only have a couple of weeks to work with Onile and get him ready for the race. Winning that money could help pay the taxes with some to spare.

Wija saw the look in Josh's eyes and knew he was fixing to enter it. Josh grinned real big as Wija asked, "You are going to enter it ain't ya?" Josh said; "Why not, we need the money and Onile can win. Beside he said you are going to be the second rider."

Wija looked at Josh as if the bump on his head had made him dizzy. "Josh you don't even know who is entering that race and you know people ain't gonna like a colored man riding in the race!"

"Don't matter," Josh said; "We can try."

Wija was pondering and then asked about how Josh would get the money to enter the race. It is almost three weeks away Josh said as he pointed to the words on the bottom of the sheet which was printed, "Pay entry fee on Race Day." I will talk to mom.

Wija laughed, I want to see that. "We have some work to do if we are going to race. Onile will need to be trained. It will be good for Tim too. He use to train horses for running and will know what to do in preparing him."

"We have two things going for us, Josh said. "Tim knows what to train for and expect and we have the fastest horse that I have ever been on." Josh entered the store and signed up for the race. He noticed that two horses had already been entered, one from Selma and the other from the Ruffkin plantation. This was going to be interesting. Josh had never been in a race before but was excited about the chance. He verified with the store owner Mr. Bullard that Wija would be allowed to ride the first half of the race. Mr. Bullard agreed and made sure it was noted on the entry form and approved by him. Mr. Bullard owned half the buildings in the town of Jackson. Getting his approval was important because no one would question him or his decision.

They went back by the Sheriffs Office but he still wasn't there. Josh left a note to Dunkin about the missing cattle and headed back to the ranch. On their way out of town they tried to judge the distance from the middle of town to the big oak. As they reached the oak tree they looked back and could see that the edge of town, guessing that it was about a half a mile away. The road had a slow downgrade for about two hundred yards from the outskirts of town then the road leveled off. Going back, the run would be slightly up hill. That may be good for Onile since he was use to fleeing the cavalry horses through hills. Josh thought about the prize money and how if they won the race, it would help with the taxes. It was well worth the try and he felt that Onile could win.

They started down the road talking about training the horse. At first they felt a change in the air and shaking of the ground. They then could hear the sound of an explosion. Hey turned around to look back at Jackson and could see a large cloud of black smoke. The explosion was loud and it shook hard enough to shake the ground where they were standing. We must go back said Wija;

someone may be hurt. Josh agreed and they headed back to the town. As they neared there was a second explosion, not as big as the first but big. There was a lot of smoke and fire at the fort. The town seemed untouched with the exception of broken windows but the north section of the fort was gone and the wall was down. Soldiers were running everywhere and town people had started a bucket brigade to help try to put out some of the fires. Josh was concerned about Ben. When they had talked earlier, the sergeant had his troops working in the area where the wall had crumbled. They tied their horses to a rail and went to that area.

There were soldiers lying on the ground, some injured, some dead. Josh began to call out Sergeant O'Rourke's name. As they got near the corral they could hear calls for help. There was a section of the wall still standing but a large section had fallen. There was a gap between it and the ground and when Josh looked under it he noticed that two water troughs were holding it off of some of the soldiers that were trapped. Josh yelled for Ben and could hear him.

"You all right?" asked Josh.

O'Rourke; "Yeah, just pinned up against the water trough." "I dove here when the wall came down."

"We will start getting these logs up and get you out of there," Josh assured him.

"That is fine," O'Rourke replied; "I ain't going no where." He still had a since of humor in a bad situation.

Most of the horses had escaped and none had been injured. Wija got the horses and Josh and he began pulling the heavy logs off of the men. The wall of the fort was built of solid pine. Each log was about twenty feet in length and weighed five to six hundred pounds each. They would pull off two or three at a time and was careful when they would reach someone trapped. It took awhile but they finally made to Sergeant O'Rourke and got him out. He had a few scratches but was not hurt. He began to help them with the rest of the wall. The wall had crushed two men. After completing the wall Josh and Wija helped with the rest of the injured and putting out fires. Doc Taylor had joined the Army doctor and was treating the injured the best they could.

No one was really sure what caused the blast except that it happened at the ammunition storage building. It just exploded and no one knew how or why. The damage was severe to the north side of the fort but it was fortunate that the ammo was stored in a placed away from the soldiers barrack and civilian and family quarters. After getting an account of everyone it was found that seven soldiers had died with sixteen wounded. The blast killed five and the wall had crushed two.

It was near midnight when things settled down. Knowing Wija would not be allowed to stay at the hotel, he and Josh went to the delivery stable. They spoke with the owner and were allowed to sleep in the hay loft for the night. It had turned into a long day and both of them were tired. They climbed the ladder to the loft and lay down in the hay. It wasn't long before the sound of snoring and crickets took the night.

Josh awoke from a deep sleep as if something or someone had shaken him. He lay there for several minutes getting his bearings. The smell of the burned wood from the fort filled the air and Josh could tell that daylight was on the way, pushing the darkness out. Josh had awakened to an eerie feeling that someone was watching them and had been there with them in the loft. He looked over but Wija was still asleep. Josh eased up and pulled the colt from the holster. Being as quiet as he could he moved to the ladder and went down it to the floor of the stable. He could still feel someone watching but didn't see anybody. Josh walked over to Onile's stall and noticed that the horse had his head up and ears forward looking out the open door. Josh walked to the opening. As he looked out into the street he saw a figure of a man walk around the corner of the Gunsmith shop and within a few seconds a horse trotted off to the woods behind the shop. Not knowing who it was bothered Josh but not hearing them was even scarier. Who ever it was walked right up on Wija and him and neither of them knew about it. He didn't think the man would return but to make sure, he sat down on a stump and waited for daylight.

Wija awoke and climbed down from the loft. He noticed Josh sitting there and asked how long he had been up?

"I ain't sure," Josh said. "But someone was here with us."

Wija looked at Josh and looked as if he had lost a friend. "I thought I was dreaming," Wija said. "I saw a man in a gray coat and floppy hat standing in the loft. I just rolled over and went back to sleep, thought my mind was acting up on me. We have already been warned to be careful. Whoever that was could have got us both."

"I agree with you," said Josh. "Let's keep our eyes open. This man, whoever he was, must not have wanted to hurt us because he could have. My concern is that he got that close to us without us hearing him. We have got to be a little more carful, we don't know who might be after us."

Wija agreed and they both got the horses ready for the trip back to the ranch. What was needed now was a bath and some food.

Before leaving town they again went by the Sheriffs Office. Sheriff Dunkin was no where to be found. The explosion had caused a stir but on this morning there was a sence of quiet and loss. Nothing was moving on the streets with the exception of a dog. The ride home was one of caution as the two men continually watched the trees and road for anyone following them. The explosion and the stranger weighed heavy on Josh's mind. His dad had once told him; "death is sad but God has a reason for it, don't hang onto it or you might be the next victim of the death angel."The men that had died at the fort didn't bother Josh to much, he didn't know any of them but the stranger made him uneasy. He had the feeling that he would see him again.

Chapter 7

THE RACE

Several days passed with no sign of the stranger or problems. No cattle had been taken and things had calmed down. Josh and Wija kept their eyes open and neither spoke to Mrs. Alicia about the events that happened in town. It was something she did not need to know especially with the worries she already had to deal with. Christine had been meeting Josh often on picnics and such and they had gotten close. Mrs. Alicia agreed to let Josh have the money for the race even though she didn't feel that it was the right thing to do. Sheriff Dunkin had come by and promised that he was doing all he could to find the missing cattle or at least who was taking them. Josh and Wija were standing by the road when Dunkin started to leave.

"Sheriff," Josh said, "I have a question for you. We have cause to believe that you know these fellows that we had the trouble with at the line shack. It has been told to us that you took them to Doc Taylor's when they needed to get patched up."

Sheriff Dunkin looked at Josh as if he had been poked with a branding iron. "First off," he said; "I don't know that their injuries were caused by you."They came to town and said they needed a doctor so I showed them where his office was then I did ask them what their business was around here. Second thing is I do know them. I met them in prison up in Huntsville and they are bad, worse than I ever thought about being. Yeah, I know them and we don't need their likes around here. After they finished with the doctor I told them they needed to move on. They told me they had a job with Clarence Ruffkin. I did let them know Josh that I would be watching them. They are not my friends and I don't trust them. They are here for a reason and I aim to find out what it is so you can rest your mind. I will go after them when I can prove something.

Josh shook his hand and told him that he appreciated the sheriff's honesty. They parted ways and with what Sheriff Dunkin had said, Josh was satisfied that he was truthful. The sheriff didn't have to say anything but he did and that was important.

Josh had Wija mark off a distance that he felt was close to the length of the race. Tim controlled the training of Onile as the two young men practiced switching riders. Wija had a rough time at first getting Onile to let him ride but eventually he was accepted. Onile was put on a mixture of feed by Tim that he said would help Onile with his speed and strength. Josh and Wija was also lectured on how to race the horse, when to control him and when to let him run. Tim's experience with race horses worked well as he was able to get Onile to obey the commands of his riders and go when he needed too.

While running one afternoon Josh had just finished working Onile and was letting the horse cool down. The race was a week off and they didn't want to push him to much.

Josh saw Ruffkin coming up the road towards him. He sits there as Ruffkin stopped and greeted him.

"Nice horse you have there," Ruffkin said.

"He'll do," Josh said, "what can I do for you?"

"Josh," Ruffkin replied, "I would like for you to have a talk with your mom."

"About what?" Josh asked him but he already knew.

Ruffkin started by saying, "this land is too much for her and you to keep up with on your own and I would like to buy it off of y'all." "You could make a profit that I would guarantee. I would pay you enough so that you would be able to take care of you mom someplace comfortable so that she could enjoy her life and not have to work so hard."

"What did she tell you?" Mr. Ruffkin asked Josh.

"She is waiting on your paw to come home, and that she couldn't make that decision without him," Ruffkin exclaimed.

Josh sat there looking at him and wanted to light into him but thought better because of Christine. Josh said; "Sir if my mom says we will wait for my paw then that is what we will do." If you don't mind me asking, "Why is our land so important to you, don't you have enough?"

Ruffkin appeared agitated that anyone would ask him anything, Josh could tell by the expression Ruffkin had on his face. "The land," he said, "sits by the river and I need to build another shipping area for cotton and timber." "Your paw ain't coming back Josh and you know it. Your mom would listen to you."

Josh stared at Ruffkin and asked himself why a man with so much money and land could possible be so greedy. "Well," Josh said, "maybe my paw won't come back and then again you don't know anymore than I know as to if he will or won't." Thing is Mr. Ruffkin, "you don't stir a man's pot while he's away or you might not be asked to supper."

Ruffkin again seemed annoyed but Josh continued; "You have plenty of land on the river sir, built your new docks there or someplace else, we are not selling."

There was no way that Ruffkin could sway Josh but he wasn't willing to have the door slammed on him so he changed the subject. "How have you and my niece been doing?"

"I guess you would have to ask her sir," replied Josh.

Seeing that he wasn't going to get his questions answered, Ruffkin said, "I will be putting Liberty in the Stakes Race. He is fast and has good genes. He has a lot of speed."

Josh remembered the horse and had seen him run at the county fair. The horse was fast and just a little bigger than Onile. "Onile will have some competition then, you have a good day Mr. Ruffkin." Josh knew Ruffkin was madder than a wet hen, so he just rode off leaving him sitting there.

That evening Tim rubbed Onile down and fed him. He sat on the porch after supper telling Josh and Wija what they would need to do during the race and when the best times would be to let Onile run. They both listened and agreed to do as he told them. Following everything Tim was teaching them seemed to be working? They trained up until two days before the race and then headed to Jackson. They wanted to get there early so that Onile could be rested the day of the race. Mrs. Wilkes and Josh would be staying at the hotel while Wija and Tim stayed in a supply shed near the stable. It wasn't the best but it was all that anyone would allow.

On the evening before the festival the saloon was in full swing. The piano playing and other noises filled the streets. It all died down around midnight but Josh found himself wide awake. He left the room and went down to the stables to check on Onile. There was fourteen horses entered and he knew it would be a challenge. He stood talking to Onile and when a chill went up his spine. He was uncomfortable and felt as if he was being watched. He started looking around but didn't see anything or anyone but a couple of drunks from the saloon trying to help each other across the street. Walking back to the hotel he kept looking around. The street was quiet but he could not shake the feeling of being watched. He returned to the room and laid there in bed. He was thinking about the race and finally fell asleep.

The rustling of people moving about the streets woke Josh. He washed his face and got ready then went to the café to eat breakfast with his mom. After breakfast Mrs. Wilkes went to meet Zuri and Edonta. They had stayed at the ranch and left early to bring some of the can goods to sell at the festival. Josh walked down to the stables to meet with Tim and Wija. The morning was crisp, not cold but cool and it was a sign that summer was near its end. Tim was walking Onile around to warm him up. The race would be around noon but with the cool air it was good to have him warm. Tim was cautious of things and towns. He had not been to any town since he was beaten by that group of men in St. Stephens. The fear of the beating haunted him and he had very little trust.

It was hard to tell which horses would be a challenge but somehow Tim was able to tell. He would watch the horses as they walked around and could pick out things that would tell him if they were runners or not. After watching most all of them, he told Josh and Wija that the Ruffkin horse Liberty was there main challenge. A horse from Birmingham would be another one to watch out for during the race.

After helping Tim and Wija, Josh walked around the town. The day was a big one for Jackson, kind of like a county fair. Folks came in and sold their wares. The smell of fresh baked pies and barbeque filled the air with an occasional pop of a firecracker to make folks jump. There was plenty of food and games and lots of visiting with the folks that hadn't seen each other in a while. There were sack races, cooking and canning, shooting contest, and a rodeo. A big dance would take place at the end of the day but the main draw was the race. Some of the horses entered in the race came from as far away as Birmingham, Mobile and Montgomery. Awards would be given for the events and then people would just head home and wait for next year's festival.

Josh spotted Christine and they walked together and talked. Christine understood how Josh felt about her uncle. Josh told her of the meeting but she already knew. Her uncle came home angry and grumbling. She was sorry that there were problems between her uncle and Josh but she didn't know how to fix it. They walked into an alley and Josh got to kiss and hold her before having to go back to the stable and get ready for the race. Christine assured Josh that everything would be alright, wished him luck and headed for the start-finish line.

Onile was ready. Wija was riding him the first leg of the race and had climbed on him to loosen him up. All the riders were called to the entrance of the stable and Mr. Bullard read the rules of the race too them. The riders for the second leg of the race then loaded into wagons and headed out to the big oak. Onile was frisky and acted as if he knew what was fixing to happen. As the wagons were pulling off, Josh noticed Liberty and the rider. He had the same build as one of the men at the line shack. He also had a wrap around his right hand. The other rider for Ruffkin's horse sounded like the rider that had left before the other men tried to hang Tim. Josh wasn't sure but he had a feeling and his feelings were seldom wrong. The wagons made it to the oak and the riders unloaded.

Wija was nervous being the only black man in the race. He looked at the other riders and knew he would have to keep his eyes open. One rider came by and said "boy you stay on that horse, wouldn't want you to fall off and get hurt." Wija, being of a temper couldn't hold back. "Mister," he said, "When I get off this horse it will be at the big oak tree but you want see that because you will be

peering through the dust this horse has left ahead of you."
"It is what it is mister, will see you after the race."

A rope had been stretched across the street and the fourteen riders walked their horses up to it. The sun was beaming down and the coolness of the morning had long gone and changed to the sight of heat devils dancing on the road. People had lined both sides of the street and sidewalks out past the edge of town. Folks were standing on balconies and on roof tops for a better view of the race. A lookout had been spotted on the edge of town to signal when the horses would be making their return. Everything was set and it was now all left up to Onile to do what it was felt he could do best, run.

Horses were fidgeting at the rope in anticipation. Liberty was in the middle of the street. Onile was placed on the out side because of Wija. Mr. Bullard didn't want him in the middle because he felt that it would be a bad place for Wija. Onile would have to make up some ground but it was safer. Wija watched as the gun was raised and fired. The rope dropped to the ground and the horses thundered down the street. Within a hundred yards it was apparent that there would be three horses in this race. Liberty was in the lead at the first right turn into the main street heading out of town. Onile had covered ground quickly and passed the horse from Birmingham and was close to Liberty at the first turn.

As they made the turn Onile came up to the left side of Liberty. Liberties rider had a wrap around the right hand and Wija noticed it. As they straightened out in the turn and had completed the three hundred yard sprint to the edge of town, Onile came up along side Liberty. The rider had a crop in his hand and swung at Wija striking him on the arm. It stung like fire and Wija moved out away from him. Onile kept the pace even though Wija was trying to hold him back as Tim had told him to do. This horse wanted too run, he wanted to be in the front and that made it hard to hold him back. Onile again came along side Liberty and again the rider swung the crop striking Wija across the chest. Wija pulled back and fell in behind Liberty. Onile would not stay there no matter how hard Wija tried to keep him back. There was still one quarter of a mile to the big oak Wija waited and when he could see the tree he brought Onile up to the right side of Liberty. He figured the rider wouldn't be able to use the injured hand to strike him with the crop. Another horse had caught them and was just off the flank of Liberty. The horse moved to the right and was following Onile. The rider shoved Liberty over to the right and began to slowly move Onile over to the edge of the road. A large tree had fallen off of the edge of the road and the trunk was sitting about four feet off of the ground. It didn't take long for Wija to figure out what the Ruffkin rider was doing. Wija tried to move Onile back to the left but Liberty was just too big to move over. Wija moved back to the right and let Onile go. The horse jumped the trunk of that tree and never missed a step. Wija grabbed onto his mane and the saddle and held on for all he was worth. The rider behind him was not that lucky. The horse did make it over the tree but the rider was sent over the horses head and into the field near the woods.

The jump had cost Wija about five horse lengths but he was catching up. There was a slight curve to the left and as they came around the curve the oak tree was there and Josh was waiting. The riders of Liberty were changing out and the horse headed out when Wija hit the ground. Onile delayed for only a second as Josh threw his leg over the horse and found his stirrups on the way back to town. Josh had watched what happened to Wija and wanted to get close enough to take the race in town. He heard Wija yell at him to watch his self as he headed out. "They are not being fair" said Wija. Josh lifted his hand to acknowledge that he understood.

All the other horses started to come in and there was a commotion with them changing riders.

Wija walked over to the rider that had struck him with the crop. "You broke rules," Wija said to the man.

"You just need to ride better or find something else to do," the man said.

Wija looked at him and smiled, "I do know how to do something else" he said. Wija looked around and noticed everyone was looking the other way.

"Yeah what is that boy?" said the man with his back to Wija.

"Fight" Wija said; He grabbed the man by the shoulder and spun him around, his right fist struck the man square in the jaw. The man hit the ground like a sack of feed. Wija walked back up into the group watching the race. No one noticed what had happened.

One fellow looked around and said; "Hey what happened to Duke? Wija looked around as if he was surprised and said, "Seems the race may have been a little tough on him." Wija climbed into the wagon for the ride back to town, smiling to himself as they loaded Duke into the wagon.

Josh was a short distance behind when he saw the slow grade of the hill that led back to town. Liberties rider kept looking back. Onile was catching up but Josh was holding him back to keep him from tiring out. As they came up the hill Josh was scanning the roof tops and spotted Tim. He was waving a white scarf which was the signal to let Onile go. Josh did and when Onile felt the pressure on the reins release, he went faster. Onile caught Liberty at the top of the hill just as they entered town. They ran side by side for about fifty yards then Onile pulled away. The slight hill had taken the energy that Liberty had and he was losing ground. Turning left back towards the finish line Josh could feel Onile surging. He was not weakening but getting stronger.

Two hundred yards to go and the big man they called James decided to try and spook the horse. He stepped out into the street as if he was attempting to cross it. He acted as if he fell right in Oniles path hoping that Josh would pull him up. Josh didn't stop and Onile didn't either. James saw that they were not going to stop and could only curl up into a ball. Onile simply jumped over him.

Josh and Onile crossed the finish line four or five lengths ahead of Liberty leaving no doubt who won the race. The crowd was cheering as Josh slowed the horse to a walk and was greeted by Christine and Tim. "You were wonderful," she told Josh, "That was a fantastic race. I am sorry those men gave you problems."

Josh smiled and looked down the road at James getting up off the ground. "I am not," he said.

Ruffkins hired hands were not at all happy. Everything they tried failed. Messing with Wija during the race wouldn't matter. Many people were still hung up on old beliefs and Josh knew nothing would be said about what Ruffkins men had done. The money would help pay the taxes and this day would be Onile, Wija and Josh's day to celebrate. Josh knew that things were only going to get worse especially since Ruffkin had hoped not winning the race would cost the Wilkes their ranch. There was enough money to pay the taxes, buy seed for planting and give money to Wija and his family but not enough to pay someone to keep Ruffkin off their backs. That was going to be left up to Josh.

Chapter 8

THE STRANGER

Josh watched Ruffkin as he left town. There was no doubt that Ruffkin was upset about the race and did not hang around for the dance. Christine stayed but Ruffkin wasn't too happy about that either. Josh knew it was only a matter of time before he used Christine and Josh's feeling for her against him. Tim and Wija had left with Mrs. Wilkes to return home so that they could catch up on the chores while Edonta and Zuri were taking a couple of days off to rest. Josh was going to stay for the dance and collect the winnings from the race. Mr. Bullard asked Josh to meet him at the saloon after the dance and he would give him the money. Mr. Bullard had a safe there and had placed the entry fees into it for safe keeping. Ben O'Rourke told Josh that he would escort him to the bank that night and Mr. McIntosh would be there to let him deposit the money. Everything was shaping up to be a great night to celebrate and spend some time with Christine.

It was great to spend the whole evening with Christine. They talked a lot but little was said about her uncle. While at the dance two strangers came up and offered to buy Onile. Another man just asked Josh to consider bringing the horse to the New Orleans Fairgrounds and race him. Josh thanked all of them but declined. As the evening closed, Christine and Josh had danced and talked until there were just slap wore out. Christine smiled as she wished Josh a good evening and headed towards the hotel. Josh went too the saloon to pick up the prize money.

Sergeant O'Rourke told Josh that he would be there shortly. Josh knew nothing about the saloon. He had never set foot in the place or any other place like it. As he entered the door he found it to be dimly lit and smelled like a mixture of musk and stale whiskey. There were about twelve or so men in it mostly sitting around tables drinking and playing cards. Josh walked over to the end of the bar and told the bartender he was waiting on Mr. Bullard.

James was at one of the tables and spoke to Josh so that the whole place could hear him. "Well now, you had a lucky day and that horse of yours almost ran over me."

Josh looked at him and the three sitting with him. "The way I see it," Josh said, "It was your lucky day, my horse was in a race and you was in the street. It is a wonder you didn't get killed the way you walked out in front of him with the race going on." Josh turned his attention to the one called Duke saying; "I hear tell that you couldn't take it and just flat passed out from all the excitement."

Duke stood up and said; "That colored man hit me when I wasn't looking." He was turning red and Josh couldn't help himself.

"Who else saw him hit you?" asked Josh.

"Nobody," said Duke.

"Then it must not have happened the way you said," replied Josh. "And if it did then I guess you need to keep you eyes open a little better."

Duke shoved the chair back but James grabbed his arm. James spoke next and asked Josh where his colored friend was.

"Now you fellows know he ain't here," said Josh. "Y'all treated him so bad out there today during the race he was all tuckered out and didn't have the strength to knock anybody else out."

Josh watched the reaction and was hoping that Mr. Bullard would show up soon.

James told Josh he was mighty cocky coming in there alone and running his mouth like that and again Josh spoke before thinking.

"Well," Josh said "There were four men at the line shack and it didn't bother me then." "By the way how is your shoulder?" My colored friend would love to have that knife back.

This time James stood up, "What is that suppose to mean?" he said.

Josh exclaimed, "My friend was fond of that knife and he said he would be glad to swap you the pearl handle forty five to get it back."

James acted as if he didn't know what Josh was talking about. "My shoulder is fine," James said. "You need to watch your mouth. You don't start accusing unless you know for sure."

Josh kept egging him on. "I declare," Josh said; "It matches that one you have in your holster there." Before you go getting all fired up I just want y'all to know so you can tell these fellows that next time I won't be shooting to wound.

"Why you smart mouth cuss," James said, as he motioned to some of the men from another table. They got up and slowly moved around to where they were blocking the exit from the saloon. Two others had gotten up and were standing about five feet behind him. Before Josh could move two of them had grabbed him by the arms. "Let's see how smart you are when someone knocks those teeth down your throat." "Are you accusing us of something asked James?"

"No, No, No, Not at all," Josh said. "Not at all." Josh continued, "Just figured you may know them, one has a sore shoulder from that knife I was telling you about and the other has a messed up hand like old Duke there."

James said "Well if I see anybody that looks hurt I will let them know you are looking for them but as for now you need to learn some manners." James looked back at Duke and the other man and nodded to them. It was obvious that James was sore because he would have taken his turn whipping Josh himself. Just as Duke walked up and raised his fist a voice came from the back corner of the saloon.

You fellows may want to reconsider what you are planning on here before you go roughing that man up. James turned around to see a man in a gray coat holding a shotgun. Some of you fellows over there may want to move out from behind him, indicating James. Some of the men at the bar moved. The two holding Josh had not let go of him and Duke was looking back.

"This don't concern you mister," James said. "You need to go back to that corner you came from and keep your nose out of it."

Josh was looking at the stranger but couldn't see his face. He had on a floppy hat that almost covered his eyes. He had a full beard and looked to be in need of a haircut. He was over six feet tall but thin looking. It was really hard to tell with him wearing that gray coat. He had on some old torn jeans and black calf boots that looked like army issue. He was holding a twelve gauge double barrel and had a six shooter on his side.

James addressed him again. "Mister you need to get yourself out of this and get out of here before we take care of you too."

After a pause the stranger spoke. "I guess you are looking at this situation different than I am." "See this shotgun is loaded, both barrels. The first barrel is for you. The second will be for which ever one of these men behind you is brave enough to challenge it and then I will use my pistol. Doesn't much matter after the first shot because I don't think any of the rest have grit enough to have happen to them what will have just happened to you!" James swallowed hard. The stranger continued; "I been listening back there and I agree that this young man has a mouth on him but I am none to sure that what he is saying ain't true. Besides there are eight of you and only one of him so his odds ain't that good. I am just trying to equal it up a little."

James was attempting to be brave in front of his men but it was hard especially looking down the barrel of that shotgun. "You are right mister," James said." "There are eight of us and just you and him." "Who do you think is going to come out ahead? Again this has nothing to do with you."

"I guess you will never know how it will come out," the stranger said "as he cocked the hammers on the shotgun." "See this does concern me cause "You don't go stirring a man's pot while he is away or you just may not be asked to supper."

Josh looked at the man and his jaw dropped. He now knew who the stranger was but there was no time for pleasant greetings. He watched a man in the corner ease his gun out and yelled look out. A gun shot was fired but not by the shotgun. It came from the doorway. A voice yelled out, "everybody drop the guns." It was a welcome site as Josh looked back to see Sergeant O'Rourke and two soldiers armed and aiming at men throughout the bar. A man lay on the floor not moving and it was sure that he was dead.

The two holding Josh let him go and he reached over and took back the colt that one of them had removed from his holster. James just stood there looking at the soldiers.

"What took you so long?" Josh asked Ben.

"I was finishing up my dance," he replied.

Ben said. "You fellows gather up your friend there and go bury him someplace. Don't want to see you back here tonight."

Sheriff Dunkin came into the saloon with Mr. Bullard and Sergeant O'Rourke told them what had happened. Sheriff Dunkin also told James to take his bunch out of town and not to return. They took the corpse and left. In all the excitement no one noticed that the stranger was gone.

After the bar cleared Josh met with Mr. Bullard and got the winnings from the race. The soldiers walked him over to the bank and he placed it into safe keeping. As they walked out onto the sidewalk Josh asked Ben what happened to the man standing in the bar.

Ben asked, what man, there wasn't anyone else in there.

Josh said; "The man in the gray coat with the double barrel."

At this point O'Rourke was looking puzzled and asked Josh if he had been hit on the head. When I walked in you said something about that stirring of the pot and when I saw that fellow pull that six shooter I figured he was fixing to shoot ya. That is why I shot him.

Josh was at a loss and played it over and over in his head. The stranger was there and that stranger was his paw. He knew it as well as anything but why did he leave like that. For some reason his paw got out of there. The only thing was that James and the others knew he was there and they would be hunting him.

Sergeant O'Rourke said his farewell to Josh and headed to the Sheriff's office to make a report.

Josh went to the stables and figured to get out of town that night. The moon was half full and he didn't want to be traveling the road in the daylight. Especially now that James had lost a man he wouldn't be safe anywhere and the next time he would have to pull his gun and kill James or get killed. Neither notion struck him well.

At the stable he quickly saddled Onile and was fixing to head to the ranch. He turned around to grab his bed roll and there stood his paw.

Chapter 9

JONATHAN'S RETURN

Josh didn't know what to say or do. Jonathan Wilkes looked worn and tired. His face was drawn and sunken with deep wrinkles. His eyes were dark and empty looking, his beard and hair, long and dirty looking. He appeared as a man broken by what he had been through and seemed as if the spirit that Josh had known, was gone. If the war had done anything it had taken a man full of life and emptied all of Jonathan's energy for life opening his eyes to reality.

"Paw," Josh said as he was at a loss for what to do, shake his hand or hug him. Josh stuck his hand out and Jonathan took it, pulling Josh towards him. Jonathan embraced Josh and it was then that Josh realized what a toll the war had had on his dad. Jonathan was skinny, no where close to the weight he was when he left home.

"You look well Josh," his dad said.

That would be thanks to you Paw, if you hadn't stepped in back at the saloon I would have been a lot worse looking. Those fellows were fixing to have some fun with me.

"I know," Jonathan said, "You didn't help much with those comments." It was obvious that Jonathan was looking past Josh to the open doors of the stable. He acted uneasy and as if he was expecting something or someone.

Not being able to control his curiosity Josh asked; "What's wrong paw, who you looking for?"

"I am not really sure," Jonathan said, "Just have this feeling I am being followed. Maybe nothing but I need to be cautious."

"You mean like you sneaking around and spying on Wija and I in the loft," Josh said.

"Yeah something like that," Jonathan explained. "It was odd because I came to let you know I was back but as I came in the stable there was this man standing by your horse. When he saw me he cut a shuck and headed out the back door of the stable. Couldn't really tell who he was but after giving it some thought, I felt he may be trying to find me and I didn't want them to use you to get to me." "Does that make any sense?"

Yeah it does paw but I can take care of myself.

"By what you said in the saloon, it sounds like you've been doing just that for yourself," said Jonathan. "Anyway that is for another conversation." "What do you think the man was fooling around that horse for?"

"Don't really know," Josh replied. "I had just entered the horse in the race and he may have been just checking the horse out." Makes no difference now, you are home and we will work all this out with our cattle being taken and Ruffkin wanting our land.

"Why didn't you return home right after the war ended?" Josh asked. Before Jonathan answered, Josh continued, "We have been waiting on you, especially maw. We all thought you were dead but maw wouldn't have anything to do with those thoughts. "Now you are here and hiding in the shadows and . . ." Jonathan stopped Josh."

"I will answer your questions later, right now I have got to get out of here," Jonathan said. "I need for you to get me some ammunition for these guns and clothes. Can you get them for me in the morning?"

"Sure," Josh said; "I will have to stay in town tonight and get them when the General Store opens. I was going to get out of here tonight so that bunch from the saloon can't sit and wait for me on the way home."

"You want have to worry about them for a couple of days," Jonathan said; "They will be at home licking their wounds and trying to figure out how they lost one of their own." After they get a mind set they will come looking for you and me.

"I still have the room at the hotel so I will stay tonight and get what you need." Josh said.

"Great, now do you have some extra bullets for that forty five?" Jonathan asked.

"Sure I do." Josh asked curiously; "What do you need it for?"

"My pistol," Jonathan said smiling, "It is empty."

"The gun was empty in the saloon?" Josh swallowed hard, "You mean you were facing those guys down with and empty pistol?" "What were you going to do shoot all of em with that shotgun?"

Jonathan smiled and said; "No, I didn't have shells in the shotgun either!" The look Josh gave his paw was one that no son should give his dad. "See I could hear you and Mr. Bullard talking and he said he would meet you at the saloon. I was hoping the shotgun would keep them at bay until he arrived. I was dragging things out and as soon as your Army buddies arrived it took everyone's attention off of me so I went out the back door."

"Gee paw, I am glad it didn't come to you having to shoot. You convinced them and me that you were fixing to blow some holes in folks," said Josh. "He handed his paw a hand full of bullets."

"Do you know the old shack down by Mills Creek Bridge?" asked Jonathan.

"Yes sir," said Josh, "Use to go there as a kid."

"Get the stuff and meet me there. Watch the woods and trails just in case but I believe you will be okay," said Jonathan. "I have to go but I will see you tomorrow and we can talk about things. Don't tell anyone you have seen me or that I am here. I want to be sure everything is okay and not put my family in any danger."

"Things will be fine paw but I want say anything," Josh said. "It is real good to have you back."

"It is good to be home." Jonathan was rubbing Onile on the neck, "he is a fine animal son, you take care of him and he will take care of you, I can tell just by looking at him."

"You just don't know," Josh said, while he was pulling the saddle off of Onile. "He is special and smart." Josh walked the horse over to the stall and placed him in it, securing the gate. He turned to ask his dad a question but Jonathan was gone. Damn I wish he wouldn't come and go like that. A voice outside the stable said, "Watch your mouth son, your maw wouldn't like that kind of talk". Josh smiled to himself and headed to the hotel.

Josh stopped at Christine's door and knocked. He wanted to tell her good night and was fixing to knock a second time when the door opened. Christine stood there her face glowing and her skin looked so soft. Josh stood a second then said, "You are so beautiful, just wanted to tell you good night."

"I was wondering if you would come by," Christine said. She reached down and took him by the hand and started pulling him into the room out of the hall. "Wouldn't want people talking now would we?" She smiled as Josh stepped into the door.

"Naw, we wouldn't want that." "You know you may not get much sleep tonight," Josh said.

"Well then I guess I will have to sleep a little later in the morning," Christine replied as she closed the door.

Christine kissed Josh as she never had and he could feel the excitement of holding her in his arms. She walked away from him and turned at the edge of the bed.

"Josh," Christine said." "I am sorry for what those men did to Wija and you out there today. It was wrong and I intend on saying something to Uncle Clarence about it." He seems so distant from me now and I don't know what he was thinking hiring those men.

"It is not your fault Christine," Josh said. "Everything will work out I am sure."

"You looked so handsome on Onile today," Christine said as she walked slowly towards Josh. She reached up and unbuttoned his shirt and ran her fingers across his chest. She then stepped back and pulled the straps from her gown and let it fall to the floor.

Josh looked at her beauty and stepped towards her pulling her to him and kissing her softly. It had been quiet a day with the festival and the race. Josh knowing that his paw was alive and home. The incident at the saloon was sure to stir up more trouble but for now he was in the arms of the woman he felt a need to be with. It was a whole life time in one day as they both lay down on the bed.

About two hours before dawn Josh made it to his room. He slept a few hours before the sun and street noise woke him. As soon as he had ate breakfast he went to the general store and got the supplies his dad wanted. As he came out of the store he was met by Sheriff Dunkin.

"Good morning Josh, you got a second?" Dunkin asked.

"Sure," said Josh, "What ya need?" Josh already knew but didn't want Dunkin to know it was bothering him.

Sergeant O'Rourke filled me in on most of the stuff that happened when he walked through the door. "What happened before he came in?"

Josh said "Sheriff Dunkin; those men in there had a burr in their saddle, especially that big man James. I feel like those fellows were upset about the race and were fixing to put a whipping on me till Sergeant O'Rourke showed up."

Sheriff Dunkin asked, "What about the stranger, who was he and where did he go?" That bunch of men is with James Lawson and they will be hunting him and you. The shooting was legal and all but I am afraid they will be seeking revenge.

Josh didn't want to lie to the sheriff so he kind of stepped around the story and answered the best he could. "Didn't know at the time but I was sure glad he was there," said Josh. "He saved my bacon."

"You never seen him before?" asked Dunkin.

"Not like that I mean not before last night," said Josh. "I really don't believe he would have shot sheriff," Josh said grinning, "I think he was just trying to scare them."

"It could have been bad for all of you," Dunkin said.

Josh replied; "You just don't know sir; you just don't know." Well I am fixing to head home sheriff; I have got chores stacking up on me.

Sheriff left Josh with a warning. "That Lawson bunch is a bad bunch of men Josh and I have a feeling this ain't over yet."

"Well," Josh said, "I guess we will have to see who steps up on the porch." Josh headed for the stables and looked back at the sheriff. Let me know if you hear anything sheriff?

Dunkin nodded and walked down the sidewalk.

Josh saddle Onile quickly and headed out of town. He neared the old shack and had been watching his back trail the best he could. He didn't see anyone or anything that looked suspicious. He had left town going the opposite direction from the way he usually went and circled around making sure he would stop at points to see if anyone was following. As he reached the shack he thought back of the night with Christine and wondered what she was doing.

Josh got off Onile and tied him to the picket line tied about thirty feet from the shack. A big gray with a black mane was tied to the picket line and was munching on grass. A saddle was lying on the ground by a tree and on the flap was the insignia of the Union Cavalry. A circle with the letters U S in the middle was known all around these parts and was pretty much disliked. Josh walked to the cabin and entered after calling his paw's name. No one was inside so he started back out the door and was met there by his paw.

Jonathan was wearing some soiled and dirty clothes. He had been to the creek and took a bath. He greeted Josh and asked him if he was hungry. It was past noon and Josh was getting a little hungry so he replied, "Yes sir."

"Would you mind cleaning that rabbit on the porch?" "I got him in a snare this morning. I'll get these clothes on and get rid of these things I been wearing."

Josh left the cabin and cleaned the hare. When he went back inside the shack, his paw had shaved and cut his hair. He had put on the clothes which were hanging loose on him and for the first time Josh could tell that his paw was very skinny. Jonathan took the hare and cut it up dropping parts into a pot of wild potato's and carrots. It was done in no time and the two sit down and ate. Jonathan looked as if he hadn't had a meal for a while.

Josh watched as his paw tried to fix the shirt. When he pulled it off to roll up the sleeves, Josh saw the scars on his back. They appeared to be from a whip. He also noticed his ribs showing and knew that he would get better with time but wondered what kind of torment he had been through.

Chapter 10

TELL'S OF WAR

Josh was reluctant but finally had the nerve to come out and ask. "Where have you been paw?" Mom has waited, we all have but some of us gave up on you ever coming home. She never waivered once, she knew you would be back.

Jonathan said as he stood and walked to the door to look out, "Son, I have been where no man should ever have to go." After I left your maw and you I went to Fort Fulton and was placed in the Confederate Cavalry with the Cheathams Division. First year was bad, being away and not knowing what was going on here. We had a few skirmishes but nothing real serious. We mostly stayed around the foothills in Tennessee but were given orders to move to Georgia. We were told that a Yankee general, Sherman was pushing through Georgia and destroying everything in his path. Every time we would think we were going to face the yanks, we would get orders to move again.

At a town called Calhoun, the cavalry was given orders to stay put. We were just outside a place called Adairsville. We tried to hold the Union soldiers back but there was just so many of them. Found out later that they were from the forty-fourth out of Illinois and another bunch from Minnesota. They were skilled and good fighters and we didn't have a chance. Most of the fellows I was with were either killed or wounded. About twenty of us got pinned down in a gulch and was eventually captured. Most of our horses were killed in the fight and the rest were taken by the Union Army. I didn't fire another shot in the war, but the hardest part of my war was just starting.

Josh watched as his dad moved around the room as if he was trying to get away from the things he was telling. What happened then paw?

They loaded the ones of us that wasn't wounded or injured into a box car and sent us up to Camp Chase in Ohio. It wasn't a place I wanted to be or anyone else on that train. Hell I don't even think the Yanks that guarded the prison wanted to be there.

Josh had been told about the place and some of the horrors that went on there. He couldn't picture his dad in a place like that. Over ten thousand confederate soldiers had died there. His heart sank just thinking about it.

I had worked my way up the ranks Jonathan continued; all the way up to captain. I didn't try; it was a battle field commission. Every time you turned around a ranked officer was getting himself killed. See the Yankees would look for markings and ranks on men and if they seen anything that made a man to be an officer, they would shoot them. I pulled all of my insignias just before they captured us. They would ask who was in charge but no one would tell. Then one day I was standing with a group of my men and this corporal walked by. He overheard one of my men address me as Captain. That was all it took. They went through my stuff again and this time found my hidden insignias.

That ended my stay in Camp Chase. I was put on another train and sent to where most every officer of the confederacy was sent. I went to Maryland to a place called Point Lookout. Three weeks in Camp Chase was bad but at Point Lookout, it was a whole lot worse. The place was supposed to hold ten thousand prisoners of war but this place had over eighteen thousand. There were tents set up for sleeping and usually there were more than eight of us to a tent that was meant for four. Point Lookout set near the Chesapeake Bay and was bordered by the Patomic River. It wasn't that high above sea level and some mornings we would be wading around in a foot of water. The wall of the prison was a fifteen foot high fence topped with barbwire and a galley with soldiers walking guard. Mostly black union soldiers. There was a death line that was stuck up about twenty yards from the main fence. If a prisoner stepped over that line he would be shot and left lying until they got a burial squad to come get him. I saw a few men that couldn't take it no more and stepped over that line to ease their misery.

Once they knew you were an officer they would come get you and take you outside the fence to a room. They would ask you questions over and over again about anything to do with your company. When they got tired of asking they would take you back to your tent or whip you for being insubordinate. I got whipped a lot.

"Well it don't look like they fed yawl none to good either;" Josh said.

We would get fed two times a day. They called it soup but it wasn't much more than warm water with some meat boiled in it, bread and a cup of water. We would set traps for rats and birds or anything else we could get our hands on. When the tide came in and the water was in the compound we would catch crabs to eat. You sided with a group and watched each others backs. If you didn't the other groups would steal your stuff. Starvation was a common thing but other things killed men too. You had to keep your eyes open; some men where just plain mean and would kill you for the heck of it. Typhoid, diarrhea, scurvy and smallpox took their share too.

I was told it was better than Camp Chase but I don't see how it could have been. They treated us like animals. Men died in that place every day but those that guarded us didn't care. We were a burden to them.

"That is something you don't have to worry about again paw," Josh said. "When the war was over and you were let go why didn't you come on home?"

"Well," Jonathan replied; "It was strange, one morning we woke and there were no soldiers manning the galley." You have to realize that most of the prisoners there were officers or confederate soldiers of a special interest to the north. It was funny but with all the officers there, no one could make a decision on what to do. No guards and no food. Some said it was a trap and if we crossed the death line we would be shot. No one knew the war was over and had been over for months. Finally some fellows got brave enough to cross the death line and nothing happened. Soon everyone started crossing the line. The front gates were busted open and men started flowing out of the compound. A lot of men still thought it was a trap and climbed fences away from the gate. Once they cleared the fence they heading to the wood line at a run.

I let them leave and went back to the tent. I had been talking to a soldier they brought in and we became good friends. His name was Kennedy Smith and he had lost his leg to a musket ball. He had done something that the Union wanted information about. He was questioned as much as me but wouldn't tell them anything. I couldn't leave him there. He got the infection in his leg and I stayed to try and make things comfortable for him as long as I could. He didn't last but two day and I took his body outside the compound and buried him.

I started walking and about three days away from the prison I met a union soldier in some woods. Don't know exactly where I was but I knew I was heading south. Anyway the soldier was acting all kinds of crazy. He was riding that gray you see out there. He charged me yelling and a hooping. I grabbed a tree limb and fought him off with it until I was able to get him off of the horse. He had a knife and just like me, he didn't have any bullets for those guns. We fought for a spell and he lunged at me. I moved to the side and he tripped, falling on the knife. Killed himself and I grabbed his boots, guns and that horse. He didn't have anything else on him, no money, maps or nothing, but he did have a bag of dried jerky so

I took that. I buried him best I could and after a spell, here I am.

I talked with folks along the way and found out the war was over four months before I walked out of the prison. There were a lot of questions of how I got the horse. I would tell them that he was running loose and I got him. They didn't seem to believe me so I wouldn't hang around to much after that. I stayed to the woods and have been stealing food when I could find it. I was afraid that taking that horse could get me hung so I been watching to make sure nobody has been following me.

"Paw you don't have to hide anymore," Josh said. "It is going to take some time but things are getting back to normal." I do need to ask you though; "Did you have anything to do with the explosion at the fort?"

"No son, but that big man in the saloon, James, he did." He still has a lot of hate from the war and the Yanks, I guess. I had seen him go into the fort that day. There weren't many folks around and about three of them walked right through the gate. I didn't see them set the explosion but they all came walking out of that fort in a big hurry and when they turned onto the main street, they ran to the saloon. They just got inside the door when the fort blew up. It would be my guess that they are the ones that caused it.

Josh began telling his dad what was going on and all the things that had been happening. He told him of the run in with the men at the line cabin and the cattle missing. He also told him about Ruffkin steadily asking to buy the land.

Jonathan listened and smiled a little saying, "You are right Josh, and it is time to leave the war and everything that happened there behind. I am home and I got to get back to taking care of my family. Let's go see what your maw has that's good to eat."

Chapter 11

A HOMECOMING

Onile was prancing as they rode down towards the ranch. Josh smiled at the horse as he was just showing off for the gray. As they neared the house Wija came from the back side of the house. He looked and saw Josh and Jonathan and froze there in his tracks. There was a slight breeze blowing and the heat of the day had subsided making it a nice cool evening with a few clouds in the sky. Tim came from the barn as he saw the horses coming up and met them in the yard. Wija was still frozen and hadn't moved, as if he didn't believe what he was looking at.

Zuri came from the clothes line and when she saw Jonathan she dropped the basket of clothes and went running into the house, yelling every step of the way. Edonta was coming out of the garden and had an arm load of greens. He showed a grin as big as he could, lay the greens on the porch and hugged Jonathan as he climbed off of the horse.

Alicia came walking out onto the front porch drying her hands on her apron. Her eyes settled on Jonathan as tears welled up. She just stood there looking at him and slowly stepped off the porch walking towards him. Josh was fighting back the tears as his mom and dad met and embraced for who knows how long. It didn't matter and no one seemed to mind. Several minutes passed and everyone had a chance for welcoming Jonathan home. Tim walked up and said; "Master Wilkes, it is good to finally get to meet you."

Jonathan, in the soft spoken voice that he was known for said; "Sir, I am no ones master. I serve only one master." "You are here on the ranch because my wife and son think of you as a friend and I am sure their judging of you is not wrong. What I have been told you have earned their respect and you are to me as you are to them. I am glad to be home and ready to get back to doing what I know." After greeting everyone Jonathan went inside the house. He sat on the couch and thought about everything that had happened and he knew this was his home. He watched his wife as she scurried about the house and readied supper. The smell of the food cooking was a dream and something that he never felt he would ever see or smell again yet here he was in his living room. He leaned back and closed his eyes. Alicia shook him, supper is ready she said as she took him by the hand.

Jonathan sat at the head of the table. This was his chair and place and no one had sat in the chair for three years. He was still in deep thought and looked at the faces around the table. This time there was no talk of what the guards were doing, if the soup would be served or if water would rise into the tent. This time the conversation was about things that needed to be done on the ranch and the race that Onile had run the day before. There was a little talk about the incident inside the saloon because Josh and Jonathan knew that it would upset Alicia. The one conversation that Jonathan wanted to talk about was Ruffkin and the land. The best of all was there was no talk of the war.

After supper all the men gathered at the barn. Tim talked of ways to try and catch the people that had been taking the cattle. That wasn't the only reason they met at the barn, Tim was good at making a little wine and they had eased down to the barn where he kept it hid from Mrs. Wilkes. She wouldn't approve of it and he did not want to make her mad.

After being told by Josh on what had been occurring with the cattle Jonathan had given it a lot of thought. We will set up a trap where they have used the broken fence. I want to catch them in the act, it is the best way.

"My concern," said Jonathan; "Is why Ruffkin wants us off this land. It is not for docks or shipping his goods, there is more too it. I have known him a long time and he never does anything without a reason. We must not under estimate him." Now if you fellows will excuse me, I haven't slept in a real bed in quiet a spell and I aim to do that tonight. He smiled at everyone and headed off to the house. Josh, Wija and Tim talked for a while and then all turned in for the night.

Josh awoke as if someone had poured water on him. He sat up and could feel that something was wrong. He put on his jeans and boots and went downstairs to the porch. It was quiet but he had an eerie feeling. He then could hear chickens as if they had been scared from the roost. He could hear everything and all of a sudden Tim yelled who's there? Inside the barn there was a shot and the horses were acting up. Josh stepped inside the door and grabbed his gun which was hanging in the holster. As he came back out on the porch he noticed two riders coming out of the barn and they had a horse with them. It didn't take but a second to see that they had placed a rope around Oniles neck and was leading him off. Josh was worried about Tim but seen him running out of the barn yelling to beat every breath.

Jonathan came out the door and Josh yelled to him, "They are stealing Onile." The two men fired more shots at Tim but he was behind the barn wall. Josh couldn't shoot at them because he didn't want to hit Onile so he calmly whistled and clapped his hands together twice. That was all it took. Onile jerked the saddle off of the horse that had it wrapped around the horn and sent the cowboy flying. Onile came back at a run, dragging that saddle behind him. He ran up to Josh and stopped, agitated with the rope on his neck. Josh quickly removed the rope and handed Onile to Tim as he came up. Jonathan had started towards the cowboy on the ground but he had already got on his feet and was picked up by his partner. They were off down the road and safe for now.

"Are you okay Tim?" asked Jonathan.

"Yes sir, just a little shook." "Them fella's aimed to take Onile, they must have like the way he ran that race. Word get around that the horse can run people will try and get him from ya. "It wouldn't surprise me if the same fellas come back later and try buying him since we don't know who they are."

"Where and when did you teach that horse to do that Josh," asked Jonathan.

"Been working on it since I had him paw but that is the first time he has ever came back to me."

"Damist thing I every seen," Jonathan said. "Maybe we ought to train our cows to do that he said laughing." "Well I don't think those fellows will try again anytime soon, especially not tonight. Let's go get some sleep."

Josh walked up to Onile and rubbed him on the neck. Tim told Josh not to worry; he would stay in the barn with him for the rest of the night. With that Josh headed back into the house as Tim grabbed the saddle and rope and headed back to the barn with Onile. He looked back at Josh and said; "At least we got a good saddle and rope out of it."

Josh smiled and told him, "It is yours, keep it." See you in the morning.

Chapter 12

A FRIENDLY VISIT

THE FIRST DAY home and Jonathan had his hands full but he didn't mind. The first thing he wanted to do was pay Clarence Ruffkin a visit. The return of Jonathan should stir Ruffkin up and cause him to take some kind of action. If Ruffkin was honest about what he wanted to buy the land for then he would try to purchase it like he did with Alicia. If his purpose for wanting the ranch was something else, then it would change his whole strategy and cause him to use more force to get the ranch. Either way Jonathan wanted to be ready.

Jonathan, Josh and Wija rode to the Ruffkin Plantation. The large white two storied home was large to look at. The porch ran all the way around the main structure and the road leading up to the gate was lined by massive oaks. The limbs from the oaks hung over the road giving shade from the sun and all the trees were heavy with Spanish moss. They tied their horses to hitching post and walked through the gate and up on the porch. Jonathan knocked on the screen door. A colored lady wearing an apron came to the door. She looked at the three and asked, "May I help you gentleman?"

Jonathan spoke and asked to see Mr. Ruffkin. She politely asked them to wait and went to a room off to the left. It was not odd to see most slaves still working at the ranches and plantations. They were afraid to leave them and would often stay and work for the owners unless that owner was cruel. Ruffkin didn't have a lot of slaves left. It was said that he owned over sixty at one time but his foreman and Ruffkin himself treated them bad so when all slaves were freed, a majority of his workers left, leaving him only about four or five. Most of his help now was civil war soldiers that had nothing to return to. There was a mixture of good and bad in the bunch with no way to tell which was which.

They could hear someone in boots walking towards the door. As Ruffkin stepped to the screen he paused. Looking at Jonathan he just stood there for a moment and then opened the screen door and stepped onto the porch. He shook Jonathans hand then Josh disregarding Wija. "Welcome home Jonathan," he exclaimed?

Jonathan exchanged greetings. Ruffkin asked them to have a seat and told the servant to get some tea. As she left to get them a drink, Ruffkin asked Jonathan how he had been. Before Jonathan could say anything, Ruffkin continued, "We all thought you were dead that is all except Mrs. Wilkes, she knew you would be back."

Jonathan said; "It was hard but I finally made it home." "It has been hard on everyone that was in the war and everyone here. I have seen things that no man needs to see and will dream of things that are stuck in my head. It was bad and when I get home and I hear about cattle being stolen and cabins burned. Then I hear these men work for you yet you say you don't know them. Then last night some men came and tried to steal my son's horse so I have a lot of work to do trying too get things straightened out."

Ruffkin sat back and asked, "Really, someone tried to steal that horse?" Wow, I figured to come and make an offer on him but someone must have really wanted him to try that. "Yes, I have men that work for me but I don't think they are the ones that burned your cabin or stole your cattle." I would have been told if that had happened. I don't like being accused Jonathan. "Did you get a look at the ones that tried to get the horse?"

"No," Jonathan replied, "But we have a saddle that belongs to one of them, so he will being riding bareback for a while." I don't know if they were your men or not but I will find out. If they are then I guess you and I will be on opposite sides of the fence. I don't know why after all of these years someone has decided to start taking my cattle and trying to steal from me. I can promise you one thing though, I won't be sitting around waiting for them to steal me blind. As Jonathan spoke he could see that Ruffkin was listening and the things being said wasn't making him happy.

The servant returned with the tea and gave Jonathan and Josh a glass but didn't acknowledge Wija. Josh asked her why she didn't give Wija a glass and she looked at Ruffkin.

Ruffkin looked at her and said, "If he wants a glass he can go around to the back door and she will give him some."

Josh stood up and handed his drink back to the servant. Jonathan stood and did the same. Jonathan was angry and anyone looking could see it in his eyes.

"Clarence," Jonathan said; "I went to war to fight for our right to choose what and how we wanted to govern our states. I didn't go to free the slaves because I didn't own them then and I don't own them now. Wija is a family friend and if you feel that he is not welcome to drink with us, then neither are Josh and I. To get to the point, if you know who is taking my cattle then I suggest that you warn them. I am home and I will not stand for it. That being said, you have a good day."

As they stepped off the porch, Ruffkin stood up. "Sorry you see it that way Jonathan," he said. "Josh, you stay away from Christine, she is not to be around you anymore. We will not associate with those who live with colored."

Josh turned around but Jonathan grabbed him and said; "Now is not the time we will attend to it later."

Josh looked at the door and saw Christine standing there. She was crying and spun around and headed back into the house.

Jonathan looked at Ruffkin and said; "Clarence we have been friends and it is hoped that we will be again but to separate these two because of our beliefs, well that is just wrong. This is a road I didn't want to go down but since I know most of the things that have happened I am going to have to warn you. If I find any of your men on my land doing anything that even looks funny then I will send them back to you just as the one from the saloon the other night."

"Are you threatening me Wilkes?" asked Ruffkin.

"No Sir," Jonathan replied, "Just letting you know I am aware of what is going on and I aim to stop it."

You know nothing about what is going on, Ruffkin replied, I need the land and when you settle down we will talk.

"Good day Clarence," said Jonathan.

As they got on their horses, Josh looked up and saw Christine standing in the upstairs window. She was holding a handkerchief in her hand and waved at Josh.

Jonathan saw Josh and in a way knew what was going on in his head so Jonathan offered him some words. "Son, she will be here. I can see what is in your heart and hers. She will be here when things get worked out, trust me."

"I hope so Josh," said "But it still doesn't stop the hurt that I feel."

It was the first time in Joshua Wilkes life that his heart had felt so heavy. He knew since the night at the hotel that they were meant to be together and he was not going to let Clarence Ruffkin stand in the way. He smiled at her and she turned from the window. He pictured her in his mind and for now that was all he could think about.

Wija rode up beside him and patted him on the back. "Josh she will be with you, I seen it in her eyes. She is not happy where she is and sooner or later she will seek you out and be with you."

"And how do you know this?" asked Josh; trying to hide the feeling he had. "Don't tell me this stuff about how you saw it in her eyes again."

"Make fun if you wish but the eyes tell me a lot about a person." She will seek you out. "If I am right I only ask one favor," Wija said; grinning from ear to ear.

"What is that?" Josh had smiled some and realized that Wija was just trying to make him feel better.

"That I be allowed to name your first child," Wija said.

"What is it with you and naming things?" Josh asked.

"If I name them then they will understand things as I do and help me keep you in line." You can not deny that Onile has taught you things, things that I have told him.

"Not to sure about all of that Wija and I darn sure don't want no child of mine being able to out think me. If you are right then we will figure out something and I sure pray that you are."

"It will happen," Wija said. "It will happen."

The three rode in silence for a while. They were checking the fences and riding the ranch to see what needed to be done. They were all thinking of the meeting with Ruffkin and wondering how long and what he might do.

Christine sat in her room for quiet a while before going downstairs. She was going to talk with her uncle about his making decisions for her. She was old enough and well capable of making up her own mind. As she started into the parlor she could hear voices and knew that Lawson was there speaking to her uncle. She paused just outside the room and listened.

Ruffkin was speaking to Lawson. "I don't care what we have to do, we have got to get them off that land and it has to be done in such a way as to make it look like they just up and moved. You get the Wilkes out of there and the colored will leave too."

"The only way I know to do it is kill them all and get rid of them in the river then you could take over the land at an estate sale. There would be no one left to claim the property," Lawson explained.

"No," Ruffkin was pacing, "no we can't do that." "We will just have to pick up things a little to put some fear into them. If we can get that land we will never have to worry about anything again. What's good is that don't know why I want that property. If they did I would never get them off the land. Let's just start adding to what we have been doing. Don't do anything that might draw Sheriff Dunkin out there. Dunkin has already come to me about you and those guys you ride with. He aims on keeping the peace and will do what ever it takes to put a stop to any of you." Make things look like accidents, do you understand Lawson?

Lawson grunted and was not pleased with being told what to do but he assured Ruffkin that they would do what they could. If Dunkin starts snooping around then I will handle it.

Christine listened then as they were finishing their conversation she snuck back into the library until Lawson left. She walked into the parlor where her uncle was standing. Uncle Clarence, she said; "May I please speak with you."

Ruffkin was looking out the window and she startled him when she came in. He was wondering if she had listen to the conversation and asked where she came from?

"My room," said Christine.

"Okay, what do you need?" Ruffkin asked.

"Uncle you know that I respect you and have never given you any reason to worry or think that I wouldn't do what you ask me too. Uncle I care deeply for Josh and he cares for me. I ask you to reconsider you decision about he and I seeing each other."

"Christine, you know I don't try to tell you what to do," Ruffkin said; "but for the time being I just feel that you and that boy shouldn't see each other. He seems to be finding a lot of trouble here lately and I am not sure that it is over yet. When things settle down we will talk again, now I have got things I need to do."

Christine started to say something about the conversation but decided not too. She turned and left the room as Ruffkin headed out the door. She pondered the conversation she had listened to and decided to see if she could find out what her uncle and Lawson were talking about. The one thing she knew was that she had to get to Josh and tell him but getting off of the plantation would not be easy.

Late that afternoon Christine had one of the servants ready a horse for her to go out on a ride. Her uncle had left the house and headed to Jackson. There was no doubt that he had left Lawson instructions to put someone to watch her. She felt like one of the men they called

Roderick was left to keep any eye on her. He was sitting outside the bunkhouse where he could see the front of the house. She had made friends with the servants and they all respected her. The servant brought the horse to the back of the house and she went out the back door and rode the wood line until she was out of site of the house. She rode towards the Wilkes ranch in search of Josh. As she came out of the wood line she observed Lawson and some of his men cutting through a nearby cotton field. She decided to follow them and kept hidden in the edge of the woods at a safe distance. About two miles from the plantation they turned into a gulley that the rains had washed out As she neared she tied her horse up and eased through the woods until she came to the edge of the gulley. The men were sitting around under some trees while two colored men fed about thirty head of cattle. It didn't take long for her to realize that the cows were from the Wilkes Bar Ranch as they had the brand on them. It was enough for her and she was going to see Mr. Wilkes and let him know. She worked her way back to her horse and was fixing to climb into the saddle when she was grabbed from behind. She struggled but the man was to strong for her. He grabbed her by the arm and drug her down the hill and into the gulley where Lawson and his men where. They all got to their feet as she was shoved towards Lawson.

"Well,well,well,"Lawson said."If it ain't Ms.Christine." "You haven't been following us now have you?"

Christine was mad as could be and told Lawson she had and now she knew what was going on. "You are stealing the Wilkes cattle and as soon as I can I am going to let them know."

"I just don't think that's going to happening missy," Lawson said. Let's take her back to the house and let her uncle handle this. "You have seen too much but I can't do anything with you right now. We will see what Ruffkin says and who knows maybe he will turn you over to me so I can teach you some manners. I would like that a lot, a pretty woman like you."

"Mr. Lawson," Christine said, "it will be a cold day in hell before you ever lay your hands on me and she swung her hand slapping him across the face."

Lawson grabbed her arm and looked as if he wanted to kill her right there but he just handed her off to one of the men and they tied her hands after she was placed on the horse. They left there near dark and it was night before they reached the plantation. Ruffkin was standing on the porch.

Lawson explained what had happened and was told to place a man outside the house until everything was settled with the Wilkes. I will keep her here until we get this over with Ruffkin said. "If you were not my sister's daughter, I would let them have you."

"Go ahead uncle, I have lost my respect for you now and I really don't care anymore, replied Christine. "I am ashamed that I have to be here. If my mom knew what you were doing she would be ashamed of you too."

Deep inside Ruffkin didn't want anything to happen to Christine. She was all the family he had left. He would give her time to simmer down and then try to talk to her. Christine was told not to try to leave. She wasn't going to give up trying to get a message to the Wilkes, she couldn't.

Chapter 13

MOONLIGHT MEETING

Josh rode with Wija and his dad all day thinking about Christine. He knew that the time would come when there would be a confrontation with Ruffkin and he didn't know how she would react. He was just hoping she would understand.

They checked the ranch fencing and even followed some tracks of cattle that had been taken but the tracks were hard to follow because they had been washed away or rubbed out. By taking the cattle down creeks that crossed the property, there was really no way to follow them.

As they rode Jonathan thought about the situation with Ruffkin. He had come to a quick conclusion that there was going to be trouble. He didn't like it because he didn't know exactly how many men Ruffkin had working for him or what they might be capable of. When they reached the fence that had been rigged to look like it was in place, Jonathan said; "This is where we will confront them. There is good cover here and so far they haven't been challenged here so they will think it is safe. We will come back when the moon gets up and that way we will have good light."

They headed back to the ranch and on the way they ran into Sergeant O'Rourke and three of his men. They had been out trying to round up some horses. Josh stopped and began to talk to them.

"How has it been?" O'Rourke asked.

"Been going okay I guess,: Josh said. "I would like for you to meet by paw, Jonathan Wilkes."

They shook hands and Sergeant O'Rourke said; "glad to meet you sir." "I have heard tell of you and I want to tell you sir that you have a fine son in Josh and his friend there, indicating Wija. They saved my life and even though we got off to a bad start, I couldn't ask for any better friends. I also can speak for your son's quickness with that gun, fastest I ever saw."

"Thanks, Jonathan said; "I am sure he feels the same sergeant and I am sure he owes you for the incident at the saloon. If you had not of shown up it could have been real messy.

"Why?" asked O'Rourke.

Josh butted in; "Because he was there. Remember the man I told you about in the shadows that kept that bunch from killing me, well it was paw."

"Then you were in pretty good hands," O'Rourke said.

"Yeah, you would think that wouldn't you," expressed Josh. "It is another story for another day and he smiled at his paw."

"Have you found you cattle?" asked O'Rourke.

"No we haven't but we do have a plan to see if we can catch the rustlers. We would sure like to have your company when we do if you have time," Jonathan explained. "I know there will be some shooting and with just the three of us, I ain't real sure what we are up against."

"We would like to help in anyway we can," said O'Rourke. "Just tell us when and where."

Jonathan said, "Well I was thinking tonight with the moon full would be a good time for them to come back and try again. We are going to set up around eight and hope they decide to come back."

"Would be our pleasure to help," said Sergeant O'Rourke; "We will be here around seven or a little after, will see you then."

The soldiers headed off back towards Jackson and it sure put Jonathan at ease knowing that they would have some help. As they headed back home they made plans on what to do that night. Wija, Josh and Jonathan all were thinking of what was to come and hoping that it would turn out all right.

Alicia was none to happy about them going to face the men steeling the cattle but she understood that it needed to be done. Her thoughts were of their safety especially with Jonathan just getting back from the war. Josh and Wija were young but she had no worries about their ability to do what they had too. Even so, she was concerned.

Tim was itching to go but Jonathan asked him to stay at the ranch and help Edonta take care of things there until they returned. He agreed but there was no doubt he would go if needed. The three armed themselves. Wija wasn't real sure about the guns because he preferred a knife but he knew how to use one. Josh grabbed the Winchester and his forty five and they all headed back to a spot to meet the soldiers.

Sergeant O'Rourke had brought two men with him. That should be more than enough to handle the situation. He told Jonathan that he had spoke to Sheriff Duncan and told him there may be bringing in some cattle rustlers.

"How did he act?" asked Josh.

"Concerned that we may get hurt but said he had two prisoners in the jail and was waiting on the U.S. Marshal to pick them up. Wasn't expecting him until tomorrow so he couldn't join us," said Ben.

"Where was his deputy?" Jonathan asked.

He said the deputy was gone to St. Stephens to fetch Doc Taylor for a kid that accidently shot himself with his paw's gun Ben said, "Why?"

"Just have a feeling about him," Josh said. "If they don't show up tonight then he may be the reason. I hear they spent time in Huntsville together."

"I'll be damn; you never know do you?" Sergeant O'Rourke said, scratching his head. "Nothing worse than a bad sheriff, sure hope he ain't one."

"Me too," said Jonathan.

They all headed to the busted fence and set up in the woods nearby. They were placed so that there would be no cross fire and they could challenge anyone without an incident. The crickets were chirping and a lone screech owl was cutting up in the woods. The coolness from the river was blowing in from the north and made the days warmth fade away. Everything else was quiet and nothing but an occasional rabbit would rumple through the woods.

It was nearing midnight when one of the soldiers signal that riders were coming. Everyone readied themselves. The plan was to let them get to the herd and start back before challenging them. That would give Jonathan and Sergeant O'Rourke a chance to count the rustlers and see how many of them they would be up against.

One of the riders came up to the fence and pulled the wire back. Josh knew right away that it was Duke. As they came through the opening they were counted. There were thirteen riders, an awful lot of men just to come and get a few head of cattle. This time there was more to there desire than just to take a few cattle. James Lawson was out front and stopped them just inside the opened fence.

"Okay, tonight we take every cow. I don't want any of them left on this field. Let's see what the Wilkes can do with no cattle to do anything with." The men started out to round up the cows. Lawson sat there watching and kept looking around but he felt comfortable that no one was there.

All the men that were with Jonathan stayed in the woods and waited on his signal. He wanted to challenge them himself first so they would not know how any men he had with him. Josh would stand with him and the others would show themselves when and if they could get the rustlers unarmed.

The men started moving the cattle towards the gate and about three hundred feet before they reached the fence Jonathan stepped out of the woods and yelled at Lawson.

"That will be far enough, Said Jonathan.

It was apparent that Lawson had been caught off guard and spun around to face Jonathan. There was no talking this time, Lawson yelled and drew his gun. Jonathan fired at him but missed and then headed to cover behind a tree that received a bullets fired by Lawson. The men behind Lawson headed for the gap in the fence shooting into the night. Everyone was shooting. Jonathan and Josh was trying not to hit any cattle and returning fire. Josh aimed at one of the men as he fired in their direction. The man fell from his horse and another slumped in the saddle. The rustlers had been caught unaware.

They hit the fence at a run but one spun around and headed strait for Wija. He was cursing Wija and saying "you going to die boy." It was Duke and he had a rage in him that could be seen even in the moon lit night. He fired at Wija at least four times and Wija calmly stepped from behind the tree and fired one shot. Duke fell from the horse and hit the ground. Two riders came close to an old wagon and were immediately taken from their horses by two of O'Rourke's men. The rest got away and none of the men with Jonathan were injured. The wounded rider was stopped at the fence. He had been wounded in the upper leg and could not stay on the horse. As fast as it started, it was over and there was nothing but the sound of the horses running through the woods and the smell of gun powder in the air. Soon it was still as a mouse.

O'Rourke sent a soldier back to Jackson to get a wagon. They kept the men seated in a circle and tended the wounded man the best they could. The two dead men lay there. A fire was built to help take a chill out of the air while they sit and waited for the wagon. Sergeant O'Rourke and one of his men joined Jonathan in the woods in case the rustlers returned.

Josh was standing guard over the two men that had been captured when Wija walked up and started warming by the fire. He was quiet and looking over at Duke lying there on the ground.

"What's wrong Wija?" Josh asked.

"Nothing," Wija said, "Was just wondering why a man wants to get himself killed like that."

"You didn't have a choice Wija; he was going to kill you," said Josh.

"I know," Wija, said "But it still don't feel right having to take a man's life."

Jonathan was walking up and said; "No it don't but sometimes a man puts himself in that position. That man lying there like that is something you don't need to hang onto." "If you do it will wear on you and eventually make you crazy. You have to realize that in the situation you did what you had too." "Besides I thought you didn't like guns?"

Wija looked at him and half grinned. "I don't but one of them fellows got my knife a while back and your son has taught me how to shoot so I guess I learned well. I am not as fast as him but I can shoot."

"That you can," Jonathan said.

About an hour passed before the soldier returned with the wagon. He had Sheriff Dunkin and two other soldiers with him. They loaded the dead and the prisoners on the wagon and Sergeant O'Rourke sent them back to town with the sheriff.

Before leaving them Dunkin spoke to Jonathan and Josh. "I am not shocked that this happened. My job is just starting because Ruffkin will say he don't know any of these men. You have stirred em up so be ready to shoot when you see them. They won't be coming with their hat in their hand."

"We will be ready sheriff," said Josh. "I want to apologize for thinking you may have been mixed up with them."

"I had my time on that side of the law, it cost me a wife and son," said Dunkin. "I envy your dad and all that he has accomplished. Being a sheriff I can try to protect people that can't protect themselves. It is the only way I can make things right. With that said, let me get these fellows back to jail and have Doc Taylor tend to that wounded man. I will be back in the morning."

They mended the fence and put the fire out. It was a long night and Jonathan knew they wouldn't try again, at least not now. They had lost five men and were probably at the plantation licking their wounds. When daylight came, they would start making their plans and Jonathan would too. Sergeant O'Rourke followed them back to the ranch. This was not over and he knew it so he would stay with the Wilkes until it was ended.

The men arrived at the ranch around three o'clock. Tim and Edonta were awake and tended the horses. They all tried to grab some shut eye but none of them could sleep. Alicia got up and made an early breakfast for them and after they ate they sat on the porch listening to the night and waiting for daylight. No one spoke.

Josh sat and thought of Christine and remembered words that he wrote for her. He had carried them in his pocket and opened the paper the words were written on. He had planned on giving them to her but now he didn't know if he would ever get the chance. The words were of his feelings and a hope that she could see what she meant to him:

I dreamed I went to heaven
Lord said son, you've done okay
So I'll send you back to earth
To spend just one more day.

So I returned and found two horses
I knew just what to do
I found some woods and hills to ride
Then I spent the day with you.

When I returned to the gates
Our Lord was standing there
He asked me why it was you
This day I choose to share.

Because I said all I wanted
Was to hold her in my arms
To take care of all she ever wanted
And keep her from any harm.

While thinking this Josh stopped and even the words he had wrote gave him pause and thoughts that he had not protected Christine. He looked down at the words and continued to read.

God said, I knew this all along
For you I'll send her a dove
To watch over her from now on
As a symbol of your love.

So now when you hear a coo
Coming from a dove up in a tree
You will know that my love was real
And you'll always remember me.

Josh folded the paper and placed it in his pocket. He would give it to her when and if he could. As he sat there he listened to the sounds of the night and could hear a dove cooing.

Chapter 14

A TIME OF SADNESS

Christine was awakened by the sound of horses running down the road to the plantation. She looked out of her window and saw Lawson coming to the porch. She could hear some loud talking but couldn't hear what was being said so she eased the door open and went to the top of the stairs. She knew something had happened and it was bad. All she could think about was Josh and wondered if he was hurt or dead. As her uncle and Lawson stood just inside the door it didn't take long to find out what had happened.

"I lost five men," Lawson said. "They had the soldiers from the fort with them and they waited on us. Duke was down when I left. We didn't get the cattle and now that they know so we won't have another chance to get them."

Ruffkin told him to calm down and give him time to think.

Lawson was furious, "I ain't going back to jail and I am sure by now they have Sheriff Dunkin with them. I will cut my losses and head back to Rag Swamp where they can't find me."

"Did they see you?" asked Ruffkin.

"Don't know but I would suspect they did. We didn't wear any hoods over our faces this time," explained Lawson.

"We can handle Sheriff Dunkin so don't worry about him. When we get that land then we can do whatever we want. You won't have to hide anymore and can buy what you want," said Ruffkin.

"Are you sure that this land is all worth it?" asked Lawson.

"Yes, the land is worth it and I just need the Wilkes off of it so I can prove what I was told," Ruffkin said.

Christine kept listening and Lawson calmed down.

"I aim to get them for what they done tonight," Lawson said.

"Now don't go and do something stupid, we have to try and work our way out of the mess we are in now," said Ruffkin.

"You do what you think you have too. They want be expecting anything else tonight," Lawson explained. "You want them off the land then we will get them off the land one way or another."

"We don't need any federal marshal in here poking around." "What are you planning on doing?" asked Ruffkin.

"Just wait and see. Maybe if they see we ain't playing they will give up and leave Lawson explained. All we have done so far is take a few head of cattle, now we need for them to know we mean business."

"I don't want to know what you have in mind and I don't really care for how you are thinking but do what ever you feel you have too," said Ruffkin.

Christine had listened to all she could and knew she had to get to Josh and warn him. Her uncle and Lawson had walked out onto the porch. She walked down the stairs and eased back towards the kitchen. Bell, the servant, was in the kitchen and Christine asked her if she could hear what the two men were talking about.

"Not everything missy but I listened enough to know there is going to be trouble," Bell said.

"I need you to get Edward to saddle my horse and sneak him around to the back of the house. Let me know when the horse is ready and tell Edward to be careful," Christine explained. "Don't let anyone see him."

Bell agreed and went out the back door as Christine went upstairs and changed into some riding clothes.

After about an hour, Edward was able to get a horse to the back of the house. Christine eased down the stairs and past the parlor her uncle was in. She eased out the back door and walked the horse through the rear gate and into a cotton field nearby. The man watching the house had apparently fell asleep and did not see her. She headed to the Wilkes ranch hoping she would be in time but she knew that Lawson had a good hour and a half on her. She rode as hard as she could.

Lawson rode out towards the Wilkes ranch with three other men. The ride took them about twenty minutes as they came up behind the house and barn. There was no doubt in Lawson's mind that what they were going to do could get him hung. They stayed in the shadows, watching and waiting for anyone to come near them. Lawson didn't care who. It wasn't long before they saw movement in the barn and then Tim came out heading towards his cabin.

Lawson and his men walked in behind Tim in his cabin and closed the door behind them. Tim didn't have a chance to warn anyone as he was grabbed by two men. After about twenty minutes they walked out of Tim's cabin finishing what they had started by leaving a message to the Wilkes. They went to the cabin belonging to Edonta. who was out tending cattle but his family was home.

It took Christine about a half hour to get to the ranch. When she arrived Edonta met her in the yard.

"Where is Mr. Wilkes?" she asked.

"They are in the house, he answered, I will take care of your horse Miss Christine."

Christine entered the front door and immediately began talking as the men stood up.

"They are coming here to do something awful, I don't know what but they left the plantation over an hour ago. I couldn't get out right away and had to sneak out because my uncle had men watching me. Lawson was mad and he intends on getting y'all off of this land." "He," said but Christine didn't get to finish what she was going to say.

Edonta was running and yelling, "Mr. Wilkes come quick, it is awful sir, it is awful what they have done."

Josh grabbed Christine and told her to stay put. Alicia placed her arm around Christine's shoulder and hugged her. Jonathan, Josh, Wija and Sergeant O'Rourke ran from the house to the barn. Edonta ran through the barn with the men close behind him. They ran towards Tim's cabin and what they saw sickened them.

Tim had been hung from the big oak just outside his cabin. They had beaten him bad and Wija stopped and dropped to his knees. In Tim's chest was Wija's knife with a note, "Here is your knife back."

Josh looked and tears welled up in his eyes. Tim had been an inspiration too him, teaching him about horses and how to teach them. Jonathan walked over and cut the rope as O'Rourke eased him to the ground.

Josh was so mad that he turned and started for the barn.

"Where are you going? Jonathan asked.

"Paw, Tim was my friend and he didn't deserve this." Josh said. "I am going after Lawson and I am going to kill him."

"Son, I know how you feel," Jonathan said. "We can't help Tim now by taking matters into our hands like that." "Tim wouldn't want us too. I want to kill him too but we have to wait until the time is right and make sure that what we do is legal and fair or we will be no better than Lawson or any of his men." You wait and things will work out for us. "You don't go stiring a man's pot." "You will get your chance, we all will."

Edonta had come running back from his cabin and was in a panic himself. "They have taken my family Mr. Wilkes, my family they is gone." Zuri, Enu and Adria were not in the cabin and it was torn up.

Jonathan tried to calm him and assured him they would get them back. Josh had gone from remorse and being mad to vengeful. Wija stood and grabbed his father and told him that they would be safe, that the Wilkes would help in getting them back.

Jonathan knew he had to get them calmed down and talked to them the best he could. He told them to take Tim's body to the cabin and it would be tended to later. Once you have taken care of that meet me at the house. In the war he had seen these types of acts against families from both sides. This however, had hit hard and he could tell there was a lot of anger in Wija and Josh. This time it was his family and this time he would handle it in the only way he knew how too hopefully with the help of the law but if not, the only other way he knew how.

At the house the men gathered and began a plan on how too get Edonta's family back without getting them killed, if they were not already dead. The plans were to go to the plantation but Christine told them that they would not be there. She told them that was why she had been made to stay at the house; she had followed Lawson and some of his men and found the cattle they were hiding. There is an old cabin in a gulch that was used by workers. She could almost guarantee them that Edonta's family would be there. Her uncle would not allow them to bring anyone to the plantation.

Josh asked where it was and she explained how to get there by going down near the river. It was just off the river about two miles north of the house. She told them to follow the road to the old burnt saw mill and there was a trail behind it that was plain to see. About a half a mile from the gulch they would need to start looking because that was where she was spotted by one of Lawson's men.

"How many men will he have?" Jonathan asked.

"He only had about eight but was joined by twelve or more when things were not going so good for them. I guess he probably has about sixteen or so," Christine said.

"What about the thirteen he had with him earlier?" O'Rourke asked.

"Some of those men were from the plantation, he probably didn't have but three of his men with him she said."

"Well that would make them outnumber us about three to one." "We will need to find out exactly where they have Edonta's family before we do anything," Jonathan said. "Edonta I need you to go to Jackson and get Sheriff Dunkin and his deputies. We will try and get there and get your family out."

"Me, Mr. Wilkes, I will be with you, I must help, I must be there," said Edonta.

Sergeant O'Rourke gave orders to one of his men to return to Jackson and get the sheriff and help from the fort. The soldier saddled and left immediately.

Everyone began to get their horses saddled and armed themselves. Jonathan saw the worry in Alicia's eyes. He tried to ease her mind at ease by telling her everything would be alright. "Alicia, I have waited a long time to get home and I don't intend on letting anyone take our land or mess with the people on this land," Jonathan assured her.

"Josh is young," Alicia said, "Even though he has grown into a man quickly, he may get too carless and that could cost him and us."

Jonathan said, "I watched Josh in the saloon and he has no fear. He knows what needs to be done and he has proven he can do it. I will be with him and he will be fine. I mean he took care of things here for almost three years and it is now time that I take back over and give him a rest."

Alicia smiled and shook her head. "I know you and Josh will come back. Just be as careful as you can."

Josh saddled Onile and spoke to the horse as if he was explaining to a man what was fixing to happen. Onile seemed to understand and rubbed his head on Josh's shoulder. The two had come so far in just a few months and they trusted each other. Josh remembered back to the first time he had seen Onile coming down the creek bank and how majestic he looked. He never thought he would be riding that same animal one day. Now this horse would take him to a fight that he may not be back from. These were all negative thoughts and he stopped thinking about it and started thinking about what needed to be done.

Christine walked up to Josh and took his arm. "You be careful, I will be waiting for you." Josh smiled at her and leaned over kissing her softly on the lips.

"Read this," he said as he took the words he had written earlier. "No matter what happens, know that I will always be near you." She took the folded piece of paper and kissed him again.

They all mounted in silence and headed towards the gulch following the directions Christine had given them. It was a good hour ride and they were all thinking about what was to come. As they got within a half a mile from the gulch they stopped.

Jonathan split the men up into two groups. Jonathan, Josh and Wija went to the north side of the gulch while Edonta and Sergeant O'Rourke went through the woods on the east side near the river. There would be lookouts, of that Jonathan was sure so they were going to try and eliminate them if they could. No shots were to be fired and no one was to get killed if it could be helped he told the group, but inside he knew it wouldn't be that easy. The group of men was badly out numbered so all they could do was try and lessen the odds against them.

Josh spotted the first lookout behind the old shack. Wija was sent to make a distraction in the edge of some woods. He grabbed some limbs and shook them making the sound of a squirrel. As he did this the man walked to that direction and met with the butt of a pistol, knocking him out. Josh tied the man up and dragged him behind a fallen tree. Two more lookouts met the same fate between the two groups so now the numbers got a little better.

After securing the lookouts Josh worked his way to the edge of the shack and looked through a dirty window. There were six men in the shack and in the corner of the room was Edonta's family. They were scared but did not appear to be harmed. He returned to his dad and told him what he saw. A signal was given to Sergeant O'Rourke and they all retreated to the woods and met at the old oak that they started from.

Jonathan explained that there were only six men in the shack, none of them Lawson, and he felt the rest would be at the plantation. Since Lawson was not there, it was hoped that his men would not be in a fighting mood if taken by surprise. The thing was they needed to move fast in case Lawson returned with more men.

Josh laid out a drawing in the dirt showing where Zuri and the children were in the shack. There was a door in the rear and one in front. It was decided that Josh and Jonathan would go through the back and try to get the family while the rest of them caused a disturbance in the front.

Sergeant O'Rourke waited until everyone was in place and walked out into the front of the cabin. He had cover behind a water well if he needed it. Wija and Edonta were concealed on the edges of the cabin and Josh and Jonathan was at the back door. Sergeant O'Rourke yelled to the men in the cabin and immediately they came out to face him. O'Rourke asked them where Lawson was and one answered, at Ruffkins. Only five came out of the cabin, leaving one man inside. He was looking through the front window and had his back to the rear of the cabin.

"I need to see him," O'Rourke said, "Seems he has some questions to answer."

While their attention was on O'Rourke, Jonathan eased open the cabin door and as quick as a rabbit, walked up behind the man at the window. He struck him on the head with the butt of the pistol and caught him so he wouldn't hit the floor and alert the others. Josh motioned for Zuri and the kids and they eased out the back door and behind a small wood shed. Since they were now safe, Josh and Jonathan walked out the front door behind the men who had stepped out in the yard with O'Rourke.

The men didn't see Josh or Jonathan. O'Rourke kept talking to them. "You fellows are in a little bit of trouble," he said.

A gruffly looking short, stout man asked, "Yeah, why is that?"

"Well I see about forty head of cattle over there and they don't belong too you. I know of a man that was killed and some of you were probably involved and there is the colored family that was taken to start with and I am sure there are some other things like blowing up the fort."

They all laughed and again the stout man spoke. "Well, seems to me Yank that those cattle are the only proof you have and since I figure you want be telling no one about them, yeah we hung the colored man and we have a family inside the cabin but I guess the most fun I had was helping blow up that Yankee fort. I am going to have a lot more fun when we string you up."

"Well," O'Rourke said, "I guess there might not be much fun in your future from a federal prison then because I aim to take all of you in."

All of the men laughed again and the stout man drew his gun and said; "Now you unstrap that holster and drop your sidearm Yank."

O'Rourke just stood there smiling and said; "If I was you men I would be dropping those hog legs because you are total fools if you think I came alone. By the way where are your lookouts he asked with a sneer?" "Now if you fellows will look around you, you will find that there are guns pointed at you from every direction and if I was you, I would drop those guns on your sides."

They looked around and spotted Wija and Edonta holding shotguns on them. Then they turned and seen Josh and Jonathan standing on the porch behind them. The stout man yelled for the man in the cabin but Jonathan advised him that the man was taking a nap. All of them dropped their guns and were lined up. Their hands were tied and all there weapons picked up. The lookouts were brought from the woods and all placed in an area that was easy to watch.

Edonta and Wija were glad to have their family back and safe.

Jonathan was surprised that there was no shooting and that so many men were captured without the first shot being fired. As they were standing there planning on there next move they could hear horses coming and moved all the men into the cabin. As the horses rounded the curve in the road they saw that it was Sheriff Dunkin and several soldiers from the fort.

Sheriff Dunkin was told about everything that happened and immediately turned all the men over to the Army for the explosion at the fort. Sergeant O'Rourke sent the soldiers back with the prisoners with the exception of three that he kept with him. One man that was not with the Lawson gang told them he had not helped in any of the events and that he had only arrived at the cabin that morning by order of Ruffkin. It was the first time he had seen the cattle or the family. He did hear the men talking about the killing of a colored man and said that none of the men there had anything to do with it except the man that had spoke to Sergeant O'ROurke. He said Lawson

Chapter 15

DEATH AND A SECRET

Ruffkin was coming from the barn when he saw Lawson riding up. The horses were lathered up and he knew that they had been running. There were only seven men with Lawson and Ruffkin hated to ask where the rest of the men were but he did.

"Where are the rest of your men?" Ruffkin asked.

Lawson told him not to be concerned; they were tending the cattle at the gulley. I wanted to give some of the fellows a rest so I switched them out. Why?

Ruffkin bit his lip but figured he better go ahead and tell him. "Christine is gone; she snuck out and got her horse then left without anyone seeing her. I would say she has probably made it to the Wilkes ranch and warned them about you by now."

"Well," said Lawson, "she didn't make it fast enough because we have done been there and did what we needed too."

"What did you do?" Ruffkin asked.

"You really don't want to know so let's just leave it at that said Lawson." It is late, the fellows and I are going to get some rest. Send someone to get me if you hear from your niece.

"Why?" asked Ruffkin; "What do you need to see her for?"

"Need to find out what she has told them," Lawson said. "I know she is your niece but you need to be thinking about who side she is on."

Ruffkin stared at Lawson and told him, "she has nothing to do with this and you best remember that. She is the only family I have and nothing will happen to her and I mean nothing."

Lawson could see that Ruffkin was mad so he wouldn't push it, at least not now. There was going to be a problem though because Christine was trouble for him and his men. For now he would just wait. Lawson and his men went to the bunk house.

Ruffkin entered the house and had Bell fix him something to eat. He asked her about Christine and she told him she was worried about her going off alone like she did. As they were talking, Christine walked into the back door.

"Where have you been, I have been worried;" said Ruffkin.

"Uncle Clarence, you know where I went. I went to the Wilkes ranch to warn them about Lawson and his men and to tell them where their cattle were hidden." "What Lawson and his men done over there was terrible." "Why did you hire them, they are killers?"

Ruffkin sat down at the kitchen table with his head hung down and was afraid to ask; "What did they do?"

Christine answered with tears in her eyes, "they killed the colored man, you know the one they called Tim and took the Edonta's family." "They will kill them too and the way they killed that man was awful Uncle Clarence."

Ruffkin stood up and looked at her. "Yes, I have made a mistake but all I can do is try to make it right." Bell, get Edward and y'all go stay in the quarters with Christine until this is over. I will go to the shack and see if the family is there and get them back home."

"It is too late uncle," Christine said, "the Wilkes and that Army sergeant went there with the husband and brother of the family that was taken. They went to get them and when they finish there they will be coming here."

"I am sorry Christine, I let greed take over and it will cost me," said Ruffkin.

"What are you going to do?" Christine asked.

"I don't know," Ruffkin said; "but I will think of something."

Ruffkin knew that Lawson would kill Christine and him if he could. Now get to the living quarters and stay until it is safe. Ruffkin walked to the living room and looked out the window. He was feeling bad about everything now and wished he would have thought things through before he hired Lawson. He had to make things right. He had done so many bad things in his life; he didn't want to ruin Christine's. She was all the family he had left.

Night was coming fast and there was eeriness in the air. Things had happened to Josh over the past several months that caused him concern in some aspects and happiness in others. He had the horse that he wanted in Onile, a girl he was fond of in Christine and a friend in Sergeant O'Rourke. His dad had returned and made the ranch seem like a home again. Wija and he had some close calls and learned to be men. It had been especially tough on Wija with him being colored and the deep hate of the southern people at the time, but he had handled it well and knew that he had a friend in Josh. Another thing that Wija knew was that it would get better because he said it everyday. Wija always had a positive outlook on life. He felt things would be better for all men given time for the hurts to heal and hate subside.

The good things that had happened were quite a few but the bad things just kept adding up. The worse of them was the way Tim had died. There was no cause for him having to leave the earth as he did and Josh wanted to meet eye to eye with James Lawson and hopefully make things right for Tim. The only thing to stand in his way would be his father. That may be a good thing because Josh wasn't sure he could take Lawson on and beat him in a gun fight although he wasn't afraid to try. He thought of why this had all come about, there wasn't any clear reason for it or at least none that he knew of right now. There were a lot of questions going through Josh's mind that he felt would be answered soon. What would happen was in the near future and he was just hoping all things worked out.

It was dusk when they rode up too the plantation. Ruffkin walked out to meet them and had a look on his face of a man defeated by his on actions.

Sheriff Duncan spoke first. "Clarence where is Lawson and his men?"

Ruffkin indicated towards the bunkhouse with a nod.

"You know that you will have to go with me Clarence, there are a lot of questions to be answered;" said Dunkin.

"I know," said Ruffkin. "Sheriff I have made a mistake in hiring Lawson and his men and I just want you and all these men to know that I am sorry for all the things that have happened. I didn't mean for it to happen this way. I also want to warn you that Lawson will not go with you without a fight."

"We will find out soon enough here they come," said Jonathan.

There were six of them, lot better odds than earlier in the day. As they approached they spread out and Josh found himself facing the one man he wanted, Lawson. It was obvious they had no intentions of doing anything without a fight.

Sheriff Dunkin looked at Lawson and said; "James I need you and these men to drop your gun belts and ride into town with me. You are under arrest for murder, cattle theft and the explosion at the fort. Let's make this easy James and you will get a fair trial."

"Dunkin," explained Lawson; "I ain't going back to prison and you know we wouldn't get a fair trial because all those things are true so I guess we are at a disagreement on just what to do."

Christine had come from the quarters and stepped up near her uncle. Lawson looked at her and said "You know if you hadn't been nosy we wouldn't be having this meeting right now. We would have got the Wilkes ranch, found the gold and been gone but you had to interfere with everything. Now we are going to have to kill this bunch and be on the run for the rest of our life."

Josh had listened to enough and yelled at Lawson. "The sheriff has asked you and your men to drop you weapons now I suggest you do it or let's get this over with." Josh don't know why he said it, it just came out and it made Lawson steam.

"Listen to me kid, you think you are good with that gun and from what I have heard tell and seen you are but you ain't as fast as me," Lawson said. "Now best you just wait your turn and I will get to you in a second."

Josh thought for a second then said, "Tell you what, let it be just you and I, everyone else stay out of it and we can figure out which one is better."

Christine quickly stepped forward and said, "No, No Josh. That is what he wants."

Jonathan didn't want Josh in a gunfight because he had not seen Josh pull his gun and knew that Lawson was a killer.

Sheriff Dunkin said, "ain't anybody going to draw, just have your men unbuckle their guns and drop them to the ground."

"That is not going to happen sheriff so you get on those horses and ride out of here and we will be going about our way," said Lawson.

"What gold are you talking about?" Sheriff Dunkin asked.

"You'll have to ask Ruffkin he knows the whole story," said Lawson. At the same time two of his men unstrapped their guns. Everyone started moving but no shots had been fired. "Sure hate it is come to this sheriff;" Lawson said, He was looking into Josh's eyes. Josh wasn't blinking.

Within a fraction of a second Josh saw Lawson's hand grab the butt handle of his gun and Josh moved. He fired and watched Lawson fall backward his shot hitting the ground in front of Josh. Several more shots were fired one striking Ruffkin even though he wasn't involved in the gunfight. The two men that had drawn their guns were both down as Sergeant O'Rourke and Sheriff Dunkin had drawn on them. Both of the men had been wounded but not seriously. The other three men never reached for their guns and had their hands up while being covered by Jonathan and Wija.

As quick as it started, it was over. All of them were looking at Josh in amazement at how fast and accurate he was. Sheriff Dunkin was shocked and stated, "I have never seen anyone that fast in my life."

Jonathan still had his mouth open and said "Me either, as he looked at Lawson lying there. Guess he won't be asked to supper."

Josh ran over to Christine and kneeled by her as she consoled her uncle. The sheriff took custody of the three men and Jonathan and Wija was helping carry Ruffkin inside the house. Bell was standing on the porch and yelled for them to look out. Lawson had struggled to his feet and was aiming his gun at Josh.

"You are fast kid but I want let you be a legend on my name," Lawson said.

Josh whistled and Onile spun his rear flank around and knocked Lawson to the ground. He did not get back up and died there face down in the dirt.

Clarence Ruffkin was in bad shape and Doc Taylor was sent for. He arrived and worked on Ruffkin and done all he could. He came from the room and told Christine that Ruffkin wanted to see her and Jonathan.

Ruffkin was struggling to breathe but felt he had to explain why he acted as he did and let them know he was ashamed and sorry for what he had caused.

Christine looked at him and told him not to worry about it now. We will talk about it when you get better.

Ruffkin looked at her and said, "I need for the both of you to listen, I don't have much time." Tears flowed down Christine's face as she and Jonathan stood there by his bed.

"I wanted your land Jonathan for selfish reasons and I am not even sure they were true." About seven or eight months before the end of the war I had a confederate soldier come here. He had been wounded and was in a bad way. His name was Robert Adams. He is laid to rest in the family plot. Before he died he told me how he was shot and what had happened.

There were eight confederate soldiers that had found out about a gold shipment moving by rail car from Jackson, Mississippi going to Roanoke, Virginia. They caught the train stopped near Tuscaloosa and robbed the train at night. Adams said they knew the train would be guarded but at night most of the Yankee's were asleep. They snuck in and killed the three guarding the gold and placed it on a wagon. They headed south and it wasn't long before they where caught up with. There was a shootout with six of them being killed and Adams was wounded but managed to get away along with another soldier. I don't know who he was but they did have time to hide the gold before they got caught. It was on your land Jonathan, Ruffkin said as he took a big breath, and knew it wouldn't be long. I don't know if it is true but you may want to look and see it could change your life.

"Christine this land is yours and everything here." Get Jonathan and Josh to help you take care of it, it is all I have left to give you. I am sorry for not being the uncle you needed but it is, he never finished, he then he took a deep breath and closed his eyes.

As they came out of the room Christine was in tears and Josh consoled her as best he could. Jonathan had the look of puzzlement on his face and Josh could see that something was bothering him. After Bell took Christine to her room Josh asked his dad what Ruffkin said?

We will talk about it later; you and Wija help them get Clarence ready for burial. After they had finished, Jonathan sent Wija back to the ranch to let Alicia know that they were okay and would be staying at the plantation. He also asked that she join him for the funeral of Ruffkin the next morning then they would go home and take care of Tim.

The last two days had taken the lives of five men and nothing about it seemed right. Jonathan sat in the edge of

Chapter 16

A RAINY DAY GIFT

THE NEXT TWO days was spent burying friends and family. It was sad especially having to bury Tim. He had become a strong part of the Wilkes Ranch and Josh really took it hard. The day after Tim was buried no one did anything. The day was spent sitting around and trying to relax and figure out what might be happening in the future. Josh knew that he and Christine would be closer and hopefully be able to share their life together. Wija had talked of going out west and joining the cavalry so he could help with training horses. Jonathan just wanted to forget the war and still had things on his mind which Josh noticed.

As they sat on the porch in the cool of the October evening, Josh finally asked his paw what was said the night Clarence Ruffkin died. Jonathan told him it was probably just the story of a dying man but that it had happened twice to him in the past year concerning the same story.

"What are you talking about paw, what did he say?" Josh asked.

"Well,' Jonathan started; "Ruffkin told us that he wanted our land but not for sending cotton or timber down river. He had the idea that there was gold on this land and he wanted to find it. He got Lawson to come in to try and get your maw and you off this land after your maw wouldn't sell. Lawson was going to try and take the cattle so you would not have enough money to pay taxes.

That failed when your horse Onile won that stakes race. It made Lawson mad because he had already been stuck by Wijas knife and his pride was hurt. Lawson couldn't figure out how someone as young as you could mess up his plans.

"Why would Ruffkin think there was gold on our land, asked Josh?"

Jonathan told him the story of the confederate soldier and how he had told Ruffkin that the gold taken in the robbery was hidden on this land near the river.

"Where did the soldier say it was hidden?" Josh asked with a curious look on his face.

"He didn't," said Jonathan; the soldier died before he could tell Ruffkin where they had put it. All he told Ruffkin was that it was down by the river."

Josh sat pondering and finally said; "Paw I have rode every inch of our land and up and down the Tombigbee many times. There is no place to hide anything that wouldn't be found and if they buried it we would never be able to find it."

"They didn't bury it, said Jonathan."

"How do you know?" Josh asked.

"I was told by the only confederate soldier left that helped in robbing the train. That is why he was brought to Maryland Point. They were trying to get him to tell them where the gold was hidden. Kennedy Smith, the soldier that I stayed with two days after the camp was abandoned told me a story of the train robbery and what they did and where they hid the gold. I didn't believe him because he had a fever and was dying from a leg wound that had got poison in it. I thought the fever had him messed up and talking out of his head but now I think he was telling me the truth. He wanted me to know so that I could find it."

"What did he say paw, where did he tell you they hid it?" Josh asked.

Jonathan said; "They were being chased by union soldiers and knew they had to hide the gold before they got caught up with. They came down the Tombigbee, just south of St. Stephens. They stumbled on a cave that was covered by brush and undergrowth making it hard to find. It was about midway up a hill and had two large pines, one leaning across the other like an X, crossed at the top. He said they put fourteen boxes in the back of the cave and covered them with a union army canvas."

I didn't believe him because just like you I have been up and down that river and I don't know of any place like that or any cave on our property. Now there are two men that have told of the robbery and hiding the gold in this area. It could still be on Ruffkins' land but his land is flat and I am almost positive there are no caves there. He looked as Josh stood and walked to the edge of the porch. I don't think there is on our land either.

Josh looked around at him and said; "Yes there is because I have been there."

His dad looked at him and asked him when?

"The night I was knocked out, Onile took me to a cave to get out of the weather. I don't remember much about it because I was in and out of consciousness but there is a cave. I can't remember where it is but it is near the river and on our land."

"How do we find it?" Jonathan asked

Wija had walked up during the conversation and said, "let Onile show you."

"How?" Josh asked.

"Don't exactly know how but he will show you, just think of things that happened that night and let him do as he did when he ran free. He will do as he has always done," said Wija.

Josh pulled his hat off and tapped it on his leg. I don't remember a whole lot about that night after I got hit in the head. Everything was blurred.

Jonathan said; "Okay, we may have to wait a spell but we will see what that horse knows." When you have the chance ride the river and see if you can remember anything about that night. Look for the crossed pines, If we find it then it was meant to be, if not who knows, maybe it never happened although I feel that it did.

It was near March as several months had passed and Josh tried everything he could think of to get Onile to take him to the cave. He lay on the ground, slumped in the saddle acting as if he didn't know where he was but when he did, Onile would end up at the ranch. Wija and Josh rode the river looking for the crossed pines and hill hoping to jog Josh's memory, but couldn't find anything.

Things had settled down a lot. Sergeant O'Rourke rode out to let Josh know he was going west to fight Indians. He was a good soldier and he wanted to be where the fight was so he had requested to go.

Edonta and Jonathan had settled into planting cotton on about three hundred acres of land to help take care of land taxes and were now working with Christine, helping her get workers for the plantation. She had discovered that her uncle left a large sum of money in the bank and she had plenty to help pay wages. She had decided to get away from cotton and start to plant corn on several hundred acres along with cutting timber to earn money. That left her a couple a thousand acres to raise cattle along with the Wilkes help. She also had a lot of time to spend with Josh. They had gotten closer and Josh had asked her to marry him. She accepted and the wedding would be in June.

Sheriff Duncan had turned the men responsible for the murder of Tim, the cattle rustling and explosion of the fort over to the U.S Marshall. They were all tried and found guilty and then sent to prison. He had accepted another job in Mobile and had left Jackson in the hands of his deputy.

Edonta's family had been given Tim's land so they now had fifty acres which they planted and kept food growing for the Wilkes and them. Everything had gotten back to normal, or as normal as it could with being almost two years out of the war. Colored folks still didn't have the liberties they should but with time that would happen.

Josh had not forgotten about the gold although it wasn't the most important thing on his mind anymore. Wija decided to go west and join a group of colored soldiers known as Buffalo Soldiers. They were said to be excellent Indian fighters and were all colored cavalry men. He had become interested in horses and felt he could do things to make his family proud. Josh couldn't stand the fact that he was going because Wija was like his brother.

The day Wija left, he promised Josh he would return. Josh told him he would hold him to that promise. You are as good with a knife as anyone I have ever seen and you can shoot well but I hear those Indians are good fighters so you be careful. Wija assured him he would take care of himself and come back. Wija left with Sergeant O'Rourke who had put in good words for him. It was hard to see them go but it was time for Josh to get ready for a different life with his new wife to be.

It was a Sunday afternoon, Christine and Josh had rode out to a flat grassy lea near the river to picnic. They sat and looked down a bluff at the Tombigbee passing by and talked of what they wanted to do with their life together. It was getting late and as they packed up their picnic it started to rain. Josh looked up as Onile started walking up a hill behind them. Josh clapped his hands and whistled but Onile ignored him and went through some bushes at the bottom of the hill. Josh went into the bushes after him as the rain got a little heavier. Christine followed him.

As Josh came through the bushes the area opened up to a small grass lea and then there was another slight hill with undergrowth Josh stopped and looked as Christine walked up behind him.

"What is it?" Christine asked.

Josh pointed to the two pines crossed at the top to form an X; "that," Josh said; as he watched Onile cross the lea and disappear into the undergrowth. They followed the steps of Onile and passed through the undergrowth. As they started up the hill they viewed an opening to a cave with bushes and shrubs almost concealing it from view. Josh looked at Christine, a smile coming across his face. Onile entered the edge of the cave and stood there, pawing at the ground as if he was calling them to come in out of the rain.

Josh reached over and grabbed a lightered knot as they made it to the cave entrance. They entered the cave and Josh struck a match setting the lightered knot on fire. As it burned it began to light up the cave. They walked into the cave and made their way around in the darkness. The cave had a ceiling of about twenty feet and was about twenty five feet wide. They walked to the back of the cave going seventy five feet or so from the opening before running into the back wall. As they watched from the flicker of light they found a canvas with the letters US in a circle. They pulled the canvas back and counted fourteen wooden boxes with the same stamp on them. Josh pried one of the boxes open and stepped back as he saw the reflection of the light off of the gold bars. They held each other and looked back at Onile as he stood at the entrance of the cave pawing the ground and shaking his head.

"Guess he don't like to get wet," Josh said. They both laughed as the sunlight came through the entrance of the cave.

THE END

About the Author

Eddie J. Carr, after publishing his first book, **"Truth Is", Life Love and Humor,** has now wrote a fictional tale using the southern part of lower Alabama as his setting. Like his book of poetry, he has entered history into this fictional tale that he calls his southern/western. Even though the lines do not rhyme the story told is in the same nature as his poems, full of excitement, history and imagination.

Eddie has been urged by his family and friends to continue writing and plans on beginning a lengthy story using one of his poems from Truth Is. With everything in the world as it is today, it doesn't hurt to look back at how things were. Using the struggles that people faced in a time when a person had to learn to work for them selves and use any means they could to survive.

Eddie's love of the outdoors, history and horses has brought this tale to life. His hopes are that person's reading it will enjoy the story and uncover the **"Gifts of Onile."**